GREEN ZULU FIVE ONE

AND OTHER STORIES
FROM THE VYPTELLIAN WAR

SCOTT WHITMORE

Published by 40 West Media
Copyright © 2014 by Scott Whitmore
ISBN 978-0-9886896-6-4

COVER

Norman Dixon, Jr. designed the cover. To learn more about this awesome writer/artist, follow (@normandixonjr on Twitter or take a look at his blog, www.normandixon.wordpress.com. Original cover art by Yvonne Less (Diverse Pixel)/Shutterstock.

ACKNOWLEDGMENTS

This book came about because of a suggestion made by Furman Ashley in his review of my short story "Green Zulu Five One" as it appeared in the *Space Jockey* anthology (edited by Tara Maya and available at Amazon.com). The story has changed since then, but Furman's steadfast support and encouragement have not. Thank you, sir.

For their generosity and insight, my deepest thanks go to: Tammy Salyer, Jeffrey Smith, Norman Dixon Jr., Kari Ann Ramadorai, David Lawlor, Katherine Whitmore, Lolly Caviness, and Glenda Brown. I've also benefited immeasurably from the continued support of authors Jill Edmondson and Aymen Khalifa.

Last but not least, love and appreciation to my wife, Cheryl; daughters Johanna and Katherine (I mentioned you twice!); and granddaughters Deilia, Jadelynn and Violet.

CONTENTS

Green Zulu Five One 1

The Birth of Icarus 7

Papa Sierra 10

Three Minutes Out 18

Quantam 22

Blood(i)ed 29

Ribbons and Funerals 36

Discoveries 40

A Single Step 47

Movement 54

War Stories 57

Commitment 62

A Journey Ends 69

White Oscar Four Zero 77

Shipping Over 83

Making It Count 91

Big Push 96

What Happens 104

A Promise Kept 112

About the author 119

GREEN ZULU FIVE ONE

Tyko killed the first two Vyptellians quickly enough, sending bright green streams of charged slugs into fighters that were now millions of pieces of space debris. They had been bunched up, slow to respond, and then predictable in their evasive movements — easy prey for one of the Fleet's top pilots. But the third one, that was a different story. The Vyp had experience, Tyko could tell, and the alien pilot took full advantage of his craft's superior maneuverability to avoid the pulsating green lances.

Not his first rodeo, Tyko thought. It was one of the nearly sixteen-year-old's favorite phrases, first heard in a vid about one of Old Earth's wars and explained through archive research in the base station library. A smile crept across his face as the image of a scaly lizard atop a horse flashed into his mind. The only humans who'd ever seen a live Vyp were Expeditionary Corps ground pounders, but propagandists made the most of the enemy's reptilian visage.

The Vyp twisted and turned, avoiding Tyko's slugs while attempting to gain a position to return fire. He countered each movement, both hands and feet working his craft's flight controls while targeting and status data streamed across the vid screen he faced. The sleek Vyptellian fighter, shaped like one of the arrowheads shot at Tyko's ancestors centuries ago on Old Earth, was locked in the targeting reticle in the center of the vid screen, the elongated pinlights of stars and planets on a backdrop of pure black providing visual references of the enemy's movement.

A warning indicator flashed in the corner of the vid screen and a warning tone warbled in Tyko's headset. He dismissed both with a flick of his eyes. *Not now*, Tyko thought as he closed in on the enemy fighter. The Vyp suddenly decelerated and as Tyko compensated, relaxing his finger's pressure on the thrust touchpad, the enemy fighter nosed over. Tyko followed the spiraling Vyp, holding his fire until he saw a flashing red circle superimposed over the enemy fighter.

1

Tyko grunted with satisfaction as a one-second burst sent two lines of green reaching out toward the Vyptellian. At the moment when the charged slugs should have slammed into the enemy craft the Vyp pilot again drastically slowed and evaded, spinning off to the left in a turn so violently and crisply executed that for the first time in hundreds of engagements Tyko found his jaw dropping with awe at the skill of an enemy pilot.

The warning and tone returned, brighter and louder respectively, as Tyko maneuvered to reacquire his target with a rolling turn to the left that was as sharp as his fighter's controls allowed. The Vyptellian ship reappeared on the edge of his vid screen, smaller than before but slowly moving back into the center ring where it would lock in place.

"Green Zulu Five One, you have nearly exceeded maximal battle efficiency duration. Disengage and prepare for relief." The voice of the flight control officer was calm but the tone provided no room for discussion.

"Control! A few minutes ... I need a few more minutes."

"Request denied, Five One. Disengage and prepare for relief."

Tyko maintained his course, accelerating his craft's thrust with his finger. The alien in front of him displayed skill exceeding the norm and Tyko suddenly wanted to destroy this Vyptellian more than any of the others he had faced. The engine status text on his vid screen turned red as he pressed the touchpad to coax out more speed.

"Green Zulu Five One!"

"Look at the roster, Control, see who you're dealing with. I need five minutes."

There was silence on the circuit and Tyko was sure the flight control officer was calling up the flight manifest and realizing the voice on the other end of the conversation was one of the station's top pilots.

"Five One, disengage and prepare for relief or I will order an involuntary turnover." A slight pause. "I don't give a damn who you are, son. There will be just as many Vyps to kill in four hours and you're not breaking the rules on my watch."

Tyko muttered a curse under his breath and focused on the Vyptellian as the distance between his fighter and the enemy closed. A bead of sweat rolled past his eye inside the faceshield as he stared at the vid screen, willing the red target lock circle to flash.

"Green Zulu Five One Papa, this is Control. Stand by to execute involuntary relief of Green Zulu Five One."

"Aye, Control. Green Zulu Five One Papa standing by." The voice of the other pilot was unemotional.

Tyko applied pressure to the firing touchpad but with no target lock nothing happened. Gritting his teeth, he executed a rolling turn, sending his fighter away from the Vyptellian.

"Green Zulu Five One has disengaged, ready for relief." Tyko's shoulders slumped. "On my mark, five ... four ... three ..."

His relief took up the count. "Two ... one. This is Green Zulu Five One, standing by for vector to nearest target."

Tyko's hands dropped from the controls and he leaned back in the seat, head up but eyes closed. After several moments he reached down and loosened the straps holding his feet to the control pedals. Swinging his legs to the right, he stepped out of the Fighter Control Unit (Remote), to find himself facing a small crowd of pilots and support officers, their faces upturned to get a better look at the large vid screens positioned over each control unit.

They watch the battles like my friends watched me play vid games in my parent's front room, he thought, his head slowly shaking. *No different than that.*

The pilots in the crowd were a mixture of those coming on or off watch. Pilots whose ships were destroyed by the Vyptellians remained in their control units waiting for replacement fighters to arrive at the scene of the battle. With thousands of kilometers separating the base station from the fighting, it was standard procedure to begin launching replacement waves as soon as the shooting started.

Tyko lifted the helmet off his head and tucked it under his arm as he walked through rows of control units. Slotting the helmet into a bulkhead cubby labeled with his name on a small metal plate, his thoughts drifted back to his first days as a Fleet pilot.

Fighting in Old Earth's wars was part of his family history, with one distant and long-dead relation earning the title of 'ace' for destroying five enemy flying vehicles in aerial combat (this ancestor's total of eight kills seemed laughably small to Tyko, who doubled that tally in his first week). Born shortly after the start of the war, Tyko started playing net-based space flight simulations at an early age, facing down and killing hoards of artificial-intelligence Vyps.

On his sixth birthday an e-card arrived: a greeting from the High Council praising his mental agility and lightning reflexes. His mother cried for two days. The net games Tyko loved were provided by the government and there was a good reason why the humans were always outnumbered: with a birthrate three times higher than humans, the Vyps started the war with a vastly larger population and quickly replaced their battle losses.

Tyko's draft e-notice arrived on his thirteenth birthday. Early in the war, pilots were deemed too valuable to risk in personal combat and with space-fighters relatively easy to fabricate — technology was seen as humanity's greatest advantage over the aliens — ships were redesigned to be controlled from afar. Remote combat also meant pilots could be younger.

Considered a natural fit for the program, Tyko was accelerated through the training pipeline and in just four months reported to his squadron on the base station. From the onset Tyko loved everything about his service. He lost a few fighters during early sorties but that wasn't uncommon; by his tenth mission he knew enough that it became rare for a fighter under his command to take serious damage from the enemy.

He relished every aspect of controlling fighters during space flight, seeking out and engaging the enemy. Tyko's reputation grew with every Vyp fighter he destroyed.

Life wasn't too bad off the flight deck, either. Pilots had the run of the base station with their own rec hall, a first-class dining facility, and vid center. Combat was near-constant but pilots operated on medically mandated cycles designed to keep every pilot at peak efficiency. Assisting in this were squadron support officers, older and specially selected for their mentoring abilities. Support officers ensured new arrivals acclimated to base station life and monitored the behavior and performance of experienced pilots.

Developed by necessity and refined after years of wartime experience, these protocols and procedures enabled Tyko and his peers throughout the Fleet to destroy tens of thousands of the enemy without ever seeing one.

As Tyko walked toward the flight deck hatch, he thought about having some ice cream and a nap in his quarters before returning for his next on-cycle. Passing the dark gray door leading into Primary Flight Control, known as Pri-Fly, he paused. Despite hundreds of confirmed kills, Tyko found himself bothered by the one that got away. The Vyp he was ordered to disengage from had been more skilled than any other he'd seen in more than two years.

Pri-Fly was off-limits to pilots and Tyko had never knowingly seen or met anyone assigned duty as a flight control officer. Keeping pilots and control officers separate prevented the forming of personal relationships that could negatively influence decisions. At least that was the official line. Inside squadron ready rooms rumor had it only washed-out pilots were assigned to flight control; command did not want those without the skill to fly and fight in space to mix with those who could.

Tyko stared at the Pri-Fly door, a sudden feeling of anger and bitterness washing through his body. For the past two-and-a-half years he faced thousands of the enemy and killed hundreds of Vyps. On duty two days for every one off, he logged thousands of hours in Flight Control Units, maintaining complete focus on the mission at hand while piloting fighters into combat to keep the human race from being extinguished. He did these things without question or complaint, and usually with a smile on his lips.

But the one time — the only time, ever — he asked for something, some leeway in the procedure, he was denied by a wash-out who wasn't smart enough or adept enough to make it as a fighter pilot.

Before he even realized what he was doing, Tyko's hand was on the door handle. He gave it a quick twist and shoved the metal door back. From the corner of his eye Tyko saw a support officer, her mouth dropping open with surprise, begin running across the flight deck toward him as he stepped into Pri-Fly.

"What the hell are you doing in here?" The voice came from somewhere to his left. Pri-Fly was dark as space itself after the brightness of the flight deck, the only lighting coming from rows of console screens lining the bulkheads.

"I want to know who stopped me from killing that Vyp!" Tyko stepped deeper into the room and puffed up his chest, allowing his anger to take control. "Which one of you wash-outs kept a real pilot from doing his job? Huh?"

Tyko's vision began to adjust to the dimness and he jerked to a stop, his legs suddenly numb.

Sitting at the consoles were officers who were much older

than Tyko expected, but that wasn't what sent his stomach dropping to the deck. The men and women in Pri-Fly had been gravely injured at some point. In the gloom he saw thick, jagged scars causing deeper shadows on faces, necks and arms, and each had at least one, and a few several, prosthetic limbs. The officer at the console nearest the door swiveled his seat to face the young pilot, and Tyko numbly noticed the man's detached legs leaning against the bulkhead.

He realized then these officers had experienced combat first hand, not through a vid screen thousands of kilometers from the enemy. Some of them may have been survivors of the war's first space battles, men and women who flew fighter ships against the enemy and returned with injuries Tyko and his peers did not need to fear.

More faces turned to look at the young pilot and he willed his deadened legs to move. "I'm … I'm … sorry," he mumbled as he slowly stepped back. "Please … excuse me."

The legless officer shook his head and turned back to his console as the support officer reached through the open doorway and grabbed Tyko roughly by the collar and pulled him back onto the flight deck. He barely heard her admonishments and threats of disciplinary action, or saw the faces on the flight deck turning to watch as he was chewed out.

Told he was removed from flight status until further notice, Tyko left the flight deck and wandered into the dining hall. Dropping into a seat, he looked down at a bowl of melted ice cream that had been left on the table. Tyko glanced around the room, seeing his fellow pilots alone or in groups at other tables, laughing, talking and eating. He felt suddenly disconnected from reality, as if the artificial gravity units had failed.

Suddenly, a thought came to mind.

I don't even know why we're at war with the Vyps.

THE BIRTH OF ICARUS

Taken from the Introduction of Furman's Utopia Spoiled: New Earth's War With The Vyptellians

Toward the end of the 22nd Century the peoples of Earth set aside their differences, put down their weapons, and joined together in planet-wide unity. Such political consolidation had been the ambition of dozens of tyrants and megalomaniacs throughout human history, but in the end it was achieved not because of warfare, but in spite of it.

People across the globe were tired of violence and destruction, and the divisions that caused them: religion, ethnicity, class, and political philosophy. Extremism was shunned, consensus and compromise became the orders of the day. It took time, of course. Trust was in short supply but the ancient proverb best sums up the situation: necessity is the mother of invention.

Changing the status quo was imperative.

Earth's air was poisoned by industrial processes. Large tracts of land were uninhabitable due to nuclear fallout. Temperatures were rising, and with them the oceans. Scarcities of food and drinkable water led to chronic famine. Disease was rampant and increasingly resistant to medicines developed decades earlier.

The new Earth Union made steady progress reversing the damage caused by centuries of neglect and abuse, but within two decades of unification many began to worry the population was rebounding faster than resources. Strict birth controls were put in place while at the same time serious talk began about extending humanity's reach beyond the planet. The Community Ship Project was the result.

In 2228 two fleets were launched, sending half a million humans on a search across the galaxy for new planets to peacefully colonize. Each Community Ship carried one hundred thousand men, women and children as well as animals, plants and insects — both alive and in the form of genetic code for cloning. Each ship was self-sufficient, with industrial, power generation and food production capabilities, as well as vast stores of the raw materials necessary for the creation of a new community once a suitable planet was located.

Hera Fleet traveled nearly two hundred years, on what is now known as the Long Exodus, before contact was made with the Hrustians, the first extra-terrestrial species ever encountered by humans.

An additional decade of travel lay ahead of Hera Fleet before they reached the twelve-planet system that would become humanity's new home. It was the Hrustians who suggested this system, which had three planets compatible with human life.

The planet selected to host humanity's second home in the galaxy was named New Earth, which would in time become the collective name for the colony. Although smaller in size than its namesake, there was ample room on New Earth for the travelers of the Long Exodus. Three years later, outposts were established on the other two habitable planets, Barribes and Xhialgong, the first step toward expanding the colony beyond New Earth itself.

After several years of negotiations the Hrustians agreed to transfer to humanity their technology for faster-than-light travel. This decision was not made lightly. Despite New Earth's development of advanced weapons for protection, the leaders of this commerce-minded alien race were convinced of humanity's dedication to peaceful coexistence with other species.

With faster-than-light propulsion, return travel to Old Earth took just a fraction of the time of the Long Exodus and an expedition was organized. More than two centuries after their ancestors left humanity's first home, descendants of the original Hera Fleet returned.

Old Earth's recovery had continued in the interim but many remained concerned about natural resource depletion. Nothing had been heard from Shangdi Fleet, the other Community Ships launched in 2288, so those interested in a fresh start were invited to join the New Earth colony. Two hundred million people made the trip to the colony during the next decade.

Then interest in cross-space immigration waned, in large part due to concerns that key policies of the colony's High Council were contradictory to Old Earth's Utopian Ideal. At the same time, business and industrial concerns concluded the narrow profits realized through trade between Old and New Earth were not enough to continue dedicated flights.

Travel between the two centers of humanity in the galaxy steadily dwindled until the outbreak of the Vyptellian War, when it ceased entirely. The war ended what is considered to be the first era of New Earth's history, a period of great discoveries in every facet of life as humanity sought to find its place among the greater galaxy. The next sixteen years would be a stark contrast.

Platoon Sergeant Siengha sat back and studied the new lives entrusted to her care by Command. Likely two of the five would be dead or lost to injury by month's end, if not sooner, and the rest might not see the year out. Siengha knew this not from some official report but from seeing it time and again.

The forty-three men and women of Third Platoon, Company C, 451st Regiment, 95th Expeditionary Brigade, were loaded into three air transports and headed to shore up a defensive position on the northern peninsula of the fourth-largest land formation on planet Neptec-2. The Neptec system was as much a backwater as could be found in the Vyptellian War, with each side holding one of the three habitable planets circling the medium yellow dwarf star and fighting for possession of the third.

Backwater or not, since Command decided to set up shop on the planet more than a decade earlier thousands of humans had died on the arid plains and rocky crags of Neptec-2.

In the lead transport, Siengha studied the troops around her. The newbies squirmed in composite seats which, in theory, were extruded in a shape comfortable to the average human's lower body. That theory, like so much of what Command said and did, was garbage. The sergeant knew this also from experience. Granted, she'd learned to sleep in the composite seats whether bone-tired or fresh from the rack. But think them comfortable? Not once.

The transport bucked a little, thermals or wildlife-evasion, causing the wriggling replacements to momentarily stop and look wildly around. Another sign of their complete newness; most of the experienced soldiers dozed off as soon as the transport launched and the rest sat quietly consumed by their own thoughts.

Siengha hoped the outpost was quiet when they landed so she could learn at least a little more about the newbies than just their names.

The replacements arrived that morning along with the

movement frag order. Their armor was clean and unmarred, their weapons and carrypacks warehouse-new. The three men and two women had regulation short hair and each was trying hard to maintain a blank expression to mask the awe and fear. But, their eyes gave them away.

Put 'em in the oldest, grungiest field gear, she thought, *and I can still find the fresh meat by their eyes.*

Siengha was five-foot-eight, average for a human but just a bit taller than most Vyps. She was lean with well-toned muscles, having come to believe early on in the war that faster was better: in close-contact fights she could land two strikes on an opponent to their one. It was something she'd proved time and again.

Her skin was a deep olive and her eyes were a brown so dark as to appear black; her nose was crooked after being broken more than once and a narrow scar ran from her left ear to chin. She maintained a stoic expression and a hard, confident edge to her voice, knowing soldiers would look to her to confirm or reject their own fears — another theory upheld in countless battles since her first.

And her first battle had been the first of the war, back when the opposing sides knew very little about each other. Just turned eighteen, she joined the military a few months before war was declared, hoping to see other planets and life forms, and accepting the Expeditionary Corps was the cheapest way to do so. Expedited through advanced ground tactics training, she reported to her division right before it shipped out on humanity's first offensive.

It was on a planet designated XO-5916c, and two days after an uncontested landing Private Siengha's platoon was tail-end Charlie — one of many archaic Old Earth sayings still used by the military — at the end of an advancing column. Now, years later Siengha could no longer remember where they were going, just that she and her fellow soldiers marched with confidence. They were told they would be out-numbered, but Command assured them their technological edge would prevail.

Human body armor would withstand most projectiles and edged weapons while the charged slugs from their own assault weapons would mow down the Vyps. Also, squadrons of Fleet ships patrolling above and batteries of long-range cannon to their rear were standing by to strike the aliens whenever and wherever they appeared.

To be sure, they were scared. They were at war with an

enemy Command said was ruthless, an alien species devoid of human qualities such as mercy and remorse. Siengha and her peers were told over and over that war meant killing: taking the life of an enemy before your own life is taken from you. Notions of fair play were meaningless in war.

The column crested a ridge and began to snake down into a shallow depression. Thick vegetation, bushes and broad-bladed grasses, covered the ground on either side of the line of soldiers. Taking in the scene as she crossed the top of the ridge — vast rolling hills bereft of any sign of habitation or life, brighter through her face shield, thanks to lumen-enhancing software — Siengha tried and failed to think of a comparable place on her home planet of Xhialgong.

Her eyes darted constantly — right, left, up, ahead, up, right, left, up ahead — as she tried to locate every sound that wasn't the dull, metallic thuds and clanks of armored soldiers moving in column or the whisper of the platoon net in her earpiece. She sipped water from the tube in her helmet but her mouth stayed dry and her tongue felt like a piece of tree bark when she licked her lips.

Yes, they were scared but they trusted their training and their equipment. They had been told what to expect, and were confident.

Then the Vyps attacked, swarming from prepared positions and spider holes in the deep vegetation on either side of the path. Later investigations blamed the catastrophe on commanders whose inexperience allowed movement of the column on an existing, and therefore predictable, route. But in the moment, when the screams of the dying mixed with the throaty roar of firing weapons, there was no thought other than for survival.

Command told them the Vyps would out-number them, but such an assessment, delivered in standard briefing monotone, did nothing to prepare them for the sheer number of gray-clad aliens surging forward. Much later, Siengha remembered hearing *so many so many so many so many* but she couldn't recall if the feverish chant was from her own mouth or over the comm net.

In those early days of the war the Vyptellians preferred close combat, their main tactic being to overwhelm and kill with edged weapons. Attached to the armor of one arm each Vyp soldier had a blade with a divided end that extended about a foot past the end of arm. One part of the blade ran straight out to a sharp point while the other curved away and back. The reptilian aliens had just three broad, flat fingers on each hand but the blade's arm-mount and split design allowed them to powerfully slash or stab at their enemies. Most also carried pistols firing energy pulses as secondary weapons and a few wielded axes or hammers.

Ignoring her fear, Siengha began to fire blindly into the mass of aliens to her right — there was no time to aim. A Vyp fell with each charged slug fired but the thick waves of aliens raced forward and in moments she and the soldiers next to her were surrounded. The humans used their assault rifles to ward off the Vyps in front of them only to fall from blows and blade thrusts from behind and the side. For every Vyp knocked aside five more surged forward — the aliens killed many of their own kind in the feverish assault — and every human who dropped meant more Vyps could attack those who remained standing.

Assault rifles and limbs broke as the men and women of the column simply disappeared beneath the waves of attackers. Alien blades hacked and jabbed at the humans, who found their armor could not withstand repeated blows and thrusts. Battered front and back, Siengha fell to the spongy ground among the bodies of her fellow soldiers. One of her arms was broken and she felt a wrenching pain in her lower back as he dropped.

Frantically, she looked up to see a Vyp standing over her; the alien's blade point came down on her chest, knocking the air from her body. Miraculously the armor held and when the force of the blow turned her sideways the blade slid between her torso and arm. The Vyps around her thought she had been impaled and moved on to find other victims. Siengha blacked out.

When she came to her senses again, the battle was over. She lay on her side, pulses of pain radiating throughout her body. Siengha gritted her teeth to keep from moaning and tried to breathe as shallowly as possible. Without looking she could sense figures moving around her and occasionally she heard the thud of metal on metal, followed by muffled screaming.

She became aware her earpiece was whispering softly, an all-nets message. She used her eyes to call up the control panel to her faceshield and mute it, unsure how well the Vyps could hear or if they knew the system was only active for living soldiers. Muting the earpiece automatically enabled the text feature and dimly lit words began to scroll on one side of her faceshield: ... SURVIVORS SCATTERED THROUGHOUT THE COLUMN. REMAIN HIDDEN. RESCUE OPTIONS ARE BEING EXAMINED ... THERE ARE SURVIVORS SCATTERED THROUGHOUT THE COLUMN. REMAIN HIDDEN ...

The young private lay unmoving for several hours as the sounds of Vyps moving around the bodies faded. Later she would learn the aliens were focusing their attention on the head of the column, removing the bodies of both species, the first demonstration of a Vyp practice that would generate debate and unease in years to come. Why take the human dead? For that matter, what about the injured? Were they taken prisoner or simply killed on the spot and disposed of with the rest?

The darkest theories held the captured and dead humans were eaten by the aliens, a concept the government and Command tried with success to suppress. The only thing Command knew for sure was the Vyps were studying their new foes, examining the human body for weak points and adapting human weapons technology for their own use. Within months Vyp soldiers would focus on the most vulnerable areas of human armor such as the shoulder, hip and knee joints; within a year the aliens would be able to disrupt human communications systems; and within two years the Vyps relegated edged weapons to backup or ceremonial roles in favor of assault rifles firing charged slugs.

All that was in a future that Private Siengha wasn't sure she would live to see while laying among her fallen comrades, nervously listening for alien footsteps and trying to ignore the pain in her arm, back and chest. Her armor included a first aid system that could inject pain medication, activated through the faceshield interface, but she wasn't sure how the drugs would affect her coherency. So she lay on the ground, wrapped in pain and fear, waiting to be told how and when she would be saved.

Finally the scrolling alert disappeared, replaced a short time later with a long message explaining the plan the higher-ups had come up with. One minute after the given signal, a two-minute cannonade would blanket the area with projectiles fused to deploy charged slugs parallel to and four feet above the ground — killing patrolling Vyps while (hopefully) not harming the surviving (and assumed to be prone) humans. After the initial cannonade, survivors had one minute to exfiltrate along the column's line of advance before a second round of cannon fire to deal with any Vyps reacting to the survivor's escape.

The message ended with coordinates to a rally point.

Siengha read the plan with a sinking feeling in the pit of her stomach. After laying still for hours, with pain coursing through her body, would she be able to stand when the time came? Even if she could, would she be able to move quickly enough to clear the area before the second cannonade? Assuming the Vyps reacted like humans and dropped to the ground during the first cannonade, how many would survive to contest the escape?

The message looped five times before Siengha's viewscreen flashed and went blank. Then a timer appeared and began counting down from 1:00. At 0:05 she held her breath. Suddenly the air was filled with whooshing sounds and explosions; through the bright flashes of light she saw the long grass around her wave from the blast waves. She noticed the timer projected on her viewscreen had reset and was counting down the two-minute cannonade.

One minute in she began to flex her legs and uninjured arm, and faced a moment of panic when her limbs initially didn't respond. With fifteen seconds to go she carefully rolled onto her stomach and began crawling in the direction the column had come from so many hours earlier. When the timer hit 00:00 she stumbled to her feet and began running, ignoring everything except the overpowering desire to *get away*.

Siengha smiled ruefully as she sat in the air transport en route to the outpost. She was one of thirteen humans to survive that first battle — all, like her, from the end of the column; survivors from the middle and front were cut down before making it back over the rise. As far as she knew, she was the only soldier from the ambush still suiting up for the fight. Some were mentally finished, done with war, after that first battle. Others, like Siengha, wanted to return to the battlefront as soon as possible for revenge or redemption. Over time most of the ones who wanted to go back were killed or wounded in action and moved into rear-echelon postings.

All except her.

She redeemed herself in her own eyes the next time she faced the Vyps, and in several more bloody battles after that. In the process she discovered an innate affinity for warfare that was comforting and confusing at the same time. After awhile she became known as 'Siengha the Survivor' and was considered almost a good luck charm by the officers and soldiers in her new platoon. But by the end of the war's first year, as Command realized humanity wasn't winning despite killing tens of thousands of the enemy, the nickname took on a darker meaning: she survived while those around her didn't.

Going on two decades later, Platoon Sergeant Siengha realized very little had changed from that first ambush. Some of the weapons, sure — more so for the aliens — but the basic business of killing or being killed was the same. And they fought on the same planets, capturing and losing the same ground over and over. In sixteen years, neither side had advanced beyond a wide, arcing belt of systems dividing humanity from its alien enemy.

One thing that had changed was her role in the war. She became a leader, first of a fire team, then a squad, and eventually Siengha was promoted to platoon sergeant — Papa Sierra. At first she was uncomfortable with being responsible for the lives of others, but in time Siengha realized her knowledge and experience was the best hope they had for survival.

Siengha eyed the five replacements sitting around her in the transport, their unblemished armor and close-cropped hair a stark contrast to the worn equipment and shaggy manes of the rest of the platoon. Personally, as long as they fought well Siengha didn't care how long their hair was.

She kept her own close cropped and had done so since that first battle on XO-5916c. After reaching the safety of the rally point, she had collapsed to the ground and two medical techs rolled her onto her back as her body succumbed to the hours of fear. Siengha started to violently tremble and then her stomach let go, unfortunately before she could unstrap and remove her helmet. The med techs washed the sick from her face but didn't have water or the time to spend on her hair.

Days and several washings later, the odor of vomit was still in her nose as she lay in the ward of an orbiting hospital ship.

The transport banked into a course change. The eyes of her new soldiers again darted wildly around the cabin and tongues ran across unnaturally dry lips, sure tells to minds focused on dying, being maimed, or making a mistake that meant someone else would die or be maimed.

If they lived long enough, Siengha knew they would discover the more experienced soldiers surrounding them had learned to hide these same fears. But for now the newbies felt miserably alone, together. Their Papa Sierra knew this the same way she knew everything about the war.

"Three minutes out."

Ghazni grunted an acknowledgment as his eyes moved from the vid display to the datascreens surrounding it. He tensed and relaxed his fingers around the transport's control yoke and then did the same with his toes, careful not to move the pedals beneath his feet.

Scan displays.
Flex fingers.
Wiggle toes.
Repeat.

This was his routine, the way he'd first been taught to fly multi-use transports back when Fleet gave up on fighters flown by actual pilots. Now kids flew drones from displays thousands of klicks from the battle and celebrated their kills with bowls of ice cream.

Scan. Flex. Wiggle. Repeat.

Transport missions could be long and tedious, or short and scary as hell. He had an idea this one was going to be both before it was over.

"It went to hell fast down there. I'm not sure we're going to make it." From the right seat, Duška's voice over the comm was calm. They'd flown together for more than a decade, and knew each other with the intimacy of an old committed couple.

Scan.

Ghazni registered a spike in power from one of the transport's four engines. He adjusted the fuel intake, slowly drawing a finger across a touchpad on the console between the seats.

Flex. Wiggle.

He adjusted the ship's direction by applying slight pressure to the yoke and the left pedal. They were cutting across buffeting winds loaded with ice pellets on a course he wouldn't chose for anything but an emergency. The planet below, Kekona-5, was the farthest from the system's star and much of it was snow-shrouded and swept by gale-force winds, making most flights a white-knuckle affair.

18

Repeat.

There was no visual or physical feedback inside the cockpit so Ghazni relied on the displays to know when the ship was back on level flight.

"Two minutes out. They're down to half strength." Duška was the most experienced pilot in the squadron next to him, and Ghazni knew in addition to the command net she was tapped into the data feed of the unit they were trying to save. On one of her datascreens would be a list of names in green and red text, reflecting the living and dead.

They had been flying resupply, dumping off rations, ammo, and in one case a miserable-looking, and no doubt terrified, replacement soldier to various units trying to wrest the planet from the Vyps. The unit in question, a reinforced platoon, was their third stop of the day.

The report of enemy contact came across the command net while they were on the ground for their fifth stop. Ghazni and Duška shared a wry smile that said: 'We just missed *that*.' Both knew better, though. Back in the air they heard the platoon call for an emergency evac and shortly after that they were re-tasked.

Scan. Flex. Wiggle.

Ghazni was on his second campaign, third planet. It took twelve years to capture Pherios-3 and then his corps shifted to Pherios-5, adding their weight to a fight that went on another four years. After a short break to receive new equipment it was on to Kekona-5, where the battle was so new they were still resupplying from orbit.

Repeat.

The Vyps didn't put up much of a fight when they invaded, but it sounded like that was changing. The reinforced platoon they were heading to save realized very quickly they needed to be pulled off the battlefield.

"Standing by for hot zone, contested evac." That was Frost. She and Ruiz were the aircrew for the mission, stationed in the cargo/passenger compartment. Duška had them tied into the same comm channels she was monitoring, something few pilots did but was standard procedure on their ship. Frost told him once it was why aircrew rotations with them were prized, but to Ghazni keeping everyone in the loop made too much sense to forego.

The aircrew ensured the correct supplies were delivered and

often had little time to prep the pallets for offloading through the rear combat hatch. Depending on the threat, Ghazni could land the transport, hover, or fly low and slow over the landing zone. One pass was all they could make in a battlezone.

Scan.

"One minute. One minute. Charge and test fire."

The aircrew also manned the transport's self-defense weapons, large chain-guns in sidepods, and Ghazni knew they'd already be standing at their operating stations. Moments later Frost reported weapons ready; in the cockpit he felt and heard nothing.

Flex.

They were still above the worst of the weather but very soon he would push the nose down, creating a cascading list of adjustments to be made to the engines and flight controls.

Wiggle.

He had done this so many times, but no two evacs were ever the same. He'd lost ships and aircrew before, too; there was always a chance of either happening again.

Repeat.

Time for him would slow to a crawl as his fingers and toes instinctively moved over the controls, doing what was needed before the thoughts could even form in his mind.

"Thirty seconds. Down to two survivors."

He put the ship into a dive. Warning tones sounded in his headset and flashing text appeared on datascreens. He made adjustments, evaluated the impact of what he'd done, and made further tweaks.

A low-pitched warble in his left ear told him the transport was being painted by Vyp sensors.

"Firing spoofs! Fifteen seconds. One evac remaining. I say again, one survivor." Duška controlled active and passive countermeasures, decoys and transmission arrays to confuse Vyp anti-air defenses.

"Taking ground fire." Frost. She and Ruiz would return fire as soon as they identified targets.

Scan. Flex. Wiggle.

His motions were smooth, his hands and feet controlling the transport through a series of evasive maneuvers. Climb, dive, twist, turn.

Scan. Flex. Wiggle.

"Abort, abort, abort. No survivors." Duška's voice, calm and authoritative. "Abort, abort."

Without thinking he pulled the yoke back and to the side, working the pedals and increasing the thrust to send the transport into a steep, corkscrewing climb. Warning tones chimed and text flashed on his datascreens.

He brought the transport to level flight as Duška reported to flight control, far above them in an orbiting warship. Control already knew, but she was following procedures.

Scan.

The report was acknowledged and they were released to continue the resupply mission.

Flex.

Duška gave him the course to the sixth resupply drop.

Wiggle.

With a gentle nudge of the joystick, he put the transport into a slow turn.

Repeat.

QUANTAM

Twisting and turning, holding the quantam tightly in his hands, Tyko caught a glimpse of Henrik standing near the end line. More accurately, he saw a flash of green between the white jerseys and waving arms of the two pilots from the opposing squad guarding him. Leaning forward but careful to keep one foot on the polished composite floor as the rules required, Tyko threw the quantam with all his might through the screening arms.

The black spheroid zipped through the air toward the end of the court as three defenders yelled "Pass!" Reaching his long arms above his head, Henrik caught the quantam with both hands. Spinning around, the lanky pilot carefully threaded the quantam through one of the six-point openings in the end-board to the jubilant shouts of his teammates.

There were four different-sized openings in the court-wide end-board: a large circle worth three points bracketed by two six-pointers that were half again smaller. Above the three-point hole was an opening slightly larger than the quantam itself that was worth ten points.

"Score!" Tyko pumped his fist. He glanced at the digital score/time display near the midpoint line as he jogged back to the end-line his team would now have to defend. The readout showed both squads had 54 points with a little less than two minutes to play. "Tie match, everyone. Stay alert now!"

Henrik slid over to Tyko and looked down at him with a sheepish grin. "Prob'ly should've gone for the tenner but I was too excited. Couldn't move. I'm never that open near the end-line!"

"No problem. We stop them here, score on our turn and we're on to the station championship." Tyko smiled and punched the other pilot's shoulder. "Remember what they taught us at Fleet indoc: DAM it."

Tyko's mind flashed back to a large auditorium at the Fleet Academy on New Earth. Row upon row of gray composite seats rising above and facing a black lectern where a rail-thin officer of about forty stood, his one eye staring intently at the cadets.

"In war there is no 'should have.' Strike that from your vocabulary right now, cadets! There is only what you do, and what you do after! You must decide, act, and move to the next decision point! Never look back, or you will surely die. Now, say it after me: Decide. Act. Move on."

The thunderous shout of a thousand young voices faded from Tyko's mind as Henrik's smile broadened. "What's this? You're using an approved Fleet acronym? Good to see you're back to conforming."

Three months had passed since the incident in Pri-Fly, which resulted in a two-week suspension from flight operations and a series of counseling sessions. An additional week was added during the first session when Tyko asked why New Earth was at war with the Vyptellians. The support officer across the table, a lieutenant perhaps five years older than Tyko and known among the pilots as good-natured but firm, froze in his seat. After a few moments of silence the lieutenant's eyelids narrowed and a frown creased his face. He told Tyko the question was irrelevant and when the pilot opened his mouth to ask why the counselor slammed his hand palm-first onto the table and terminated the session.

Tyko returned to his stateroom, his face flushed with anger. He paced back and forth in the small space, his mind a whirlwind of thoughts. Tyko understood and accepted his punishment for violating the rule that Pri-Fly was off-limits: rules were to be obeyed. But his anger didn't stop him from wondering about the why of that rule. Why were the wounded who had fought the war's early battles kept away from the pilots? Why make him sign an oath of secrecy about what he'd seen in Pri-Fly? What purpose did it serve? For that matter, why hide what the war was about?

As his mood cooled Tyko remembered something all cadets were taught early in their training: Fleet rules didn't always make obvious sense but there was always a reason for them.

The next day he was sitting in the station library, one of the few locations permitted as part of his punishment, reading the latest news files about the war. Clearing the vid console screen, Tyko called up the archive search and typed in a query about the start of the war. His index finger hovered over the touchscreen for a moment as he pondered the words on the screen, and the implicit warning of his extended suspension. Although he was a seasoned pilot with hundreds of kills to his credit, Tyko was still a teenager, and when the flash of the anger from the day before returned he jabbed the touchscreen.

Billions of words had been written since, but there was surprisingly little to be found about the start of the sixteen-year war between the humans of New Earth and the Vyptellians. Calling up a primary school textbook he found two ponderously written lines: *While Humanity's search for a new home in the universe was undertaken with peaceful intent, the discovery of other, less-developed species at times created conflict. The unprovoked massacre by the Vyptellian race of two thousand peaceful human settlers and the destruction of a mining and scientific exploration colony on the planet Nex Altrien sparked a war between the two races that continues today.*

Re-reading these lines, Tyko vaguely remembered seeing something similar during his own school days before his draft notice arrived.

Although he now knew the event that sparked the war, Tyko was surprised to find the knowledge only led to more questions. Why had the Vyptellians attacked? Were they provoked? How long had the colony been on Nex Altrien? Prior to or after the attack, had their been any high-level discussions between the races?

Additional searches revealed no answers to these new questions.

He checked star charts and saw to his great surprise Nex Altrien was not far from his base station, which hadn't moved in the two years since Tyko reported for duty. Fleet intelligence briefs and info vids broadcast to civilians portrayed the Vyps as bloodthirsty warmongers and humans as bravely withstanding their assaults. Yet, in nearly seventeen years the aliens had not advanced into New Earth-controlled space.

Tyko shook his head, trying to comprehend it. There must have been a time, immediately after the destruction of Nex Altrien, when humanity was wide open to assault, yet the Vyps, bloodthirsty and experienced warriors, did not take advantage.

It made little sense and he returned to his stateroom with his head spinning.

Tyko soon discovered his research in the library — indeed, everything the pilots did — was logged by the squadron's support officers. They were likely in the process of adding to his punishment for continuing to pry into the war's origin, but he made the situation much worse by sending an e-note to his parents asking them what they remembered about the war's earliest days. This earned him a blistering visit to his squadron commander, who told him the e-note to New Earth had been intercepted and deleted before delivery.

She finished her tirade by adding three weeks to his suspension.

The administrative tasks he was assigned while suspended were mind-numbing and being off the flight roster meant the rec hall and vid center were off limits. Chastised and anxious to return to flight status, Tyko decided to do what new cadets were advised at the academy: never call attention to yourself. For whatever reason the civilian and military authorities did not want people looking into the start of the war, and if he persisted the penalties would get harsher and harsher.

He didn't want to contemplate what would happen if he lost flight status permanently.

In the two months after finishing his suspension Tyko worked hard to be a model pilot, following every rule to the letter. He needed several flight rotations to regain proficiency, but by the third day back he was cutting through Vyptellian formations as if he had never left. Indeed, in many ways it seemed like he hadn't left. The swarms of enemy fighters were the same, the spectators around the flight control units were the same, and the routine of on- and off-cycles was the same.

The only difference was the squadron support officers shadowing him wherever he went.

The other pilots in his squadron barely noticed his return to the flight deck. They had barraged him with questions a month earlier, curious to know what was behind the door to Pri-Fly, but he followed orders and kept silent. His punishment was all the warning the others needed to drop the matter. Although isolation was not an official part of his suspension, the others knew enough of the military — or were quietly prompted — to avoid him during his weeks away.

So Tyko did his best to quietly fit back into the squadron. Before, he had been a peer leader but in his absence others had stepped into that role. Tyko carefully navigated this new reality, accepting his unofficial demotion while doing what he could to assist and support these new leaders. When Henrik was selected to test a new model interceptor — a choice assignment Tyko thought would probably have been his just two months earlier — he joined the others in clapping the tall boy on the back and congratulating him.

It could have been his imagination, but Tyko thought his squadron commander was carefully watching his reaction during the test model announcement just before the start of the semi-final quantam match.

The quantam court was the one place where he remained near the top of the squadron's pecking order.

Each station housed four air wings made up of eight squadrons. As Fourth Wing champions, Tyko's squadron needed to beat the top team from Third Wing for the chance to play in the station championship game against the winner of the First versus Second Wing match underway on the opposite side of the rec hall.

Taking the quantam from an official, Tyko nodded at Henrik before turning to face the opposing squad on the other end of the court. "Don't worry about me," he said to the tall boy. "I'm not only a loyal Fleet officer, but I've also downed ten times the Vyps you have."

A loud buzzer from the score/time display drowned out the laughing response.

Tyko threw the quantam to the opposing squad. A white-clad player caught the spheroid, starting the clock, and began running forward behind a wall of her teammates. Tyko's squad moved toward them, the pilots trying to position themselves to block the advance of their opponents. At the midpoint line the white squad began to fan out.

The girl with the quantam suddenly stopped, yelling "Hold!" The rest of her team froze in place, their chests heaving.

By the rules the girl with the quantam had five seconds to either throw it to a teammate or begin moving forward again, although she was limited to two successive movements before having to pass. Surveying the court, she zipped the spheroid to a teammate to her right. The play was on the opposite side of the court from Tyko, who joined his teammates in yelling "Pass" before moving to new blocking positions. The new holder passed the spheroid back to a teammate near the midpoint line who passed it back to the first holder.

The attacking team had ninety seconds to score or give up possession and Tyko expected the white team to use as much time as possible.

The first girl threw the quantam to a teammate across court and took off running toward the end-line. Sensing she was going for a position to score, Tyko followed her. He had the shorter route and arrived first in the green-painted rectangle beneath the scoring circles, turning to face the girl just as she stopped short of running into him. Raising a hand high she turned to find the quantam, her ponytail of brown hair swinging just short of Tyko's nose. Her shoulders rose and fell as the girl breathed deeply from sprinting. When she looked back at him over her shoulder, Tyko studied her face and felt a sudden and not unpleasant fluttering sensation in his stomach.

Reflecting New Earth society as a whole, the Fleet's pilot corps was comprised of males and females in nearly equal numbers. They came from a wide range of backgrounds but once they donned the uniform each was an equal part of the whole; no variance from this policy was accepted. Like Tyko, every pilot at the station entered the academy at thirteen and to mitigate against the natural force that was puberty, Fleet command placed great emphasis on developing and maintaining professional relationships between the sexes. But those running the academy were pragmatic, too. The inevitable was dealt with quietly and with discipline that was not so severe as to encourage the latent rebellious nature of human teenagers.

After graduating from the Academy and reporting to base stations and other outposts, personal relationships were tolerated but only between those of proximate rank and in separate chains of command. One of the prime functions of squadron support officers was to monitor and, when necessary, alter behavior that detracted from mission performance.

To date, Tyko's interpersonal relationships had been unremarkable. Whether it was training or some nullifying supplements in the food — as Henrik, among others in the squadron, believed — Tyko thought of the other pilots as his sisters and brothers. He was closer to some more than others, like his squadron mates, but none before generated the same visceral reaction as the girl just inches from him on the quantam court.

She had a lean face with bright blue eyes that seemed to sparkle and high cheekbones that were reddened slightly from playing. There were a few freckles on either side of a nose that was straight and perhaps a bit too small for her face. Her hair was thick and pulled back although some strands were stuck to her forehead by sweat.

As Tyko watched, captivated, the girl's eyelids narrowed

slightly and a small smile formed on one corner of her lips. She seemed to move in slow motion, her arms rising and then his paralysis disappeared with the sound of the quantam thudding into her hands. Tyko started bringing his arms up to block but in a flash the girl leaned to her left and pushed past, careful not to touch him as avoidable contact would end her team's possession.

He turned to follow, the hot flush of embarrassment on his cheeks, but the sound of the quantam slamming through the end-board told him he was too late.

Hanging his head to avoid the angry stares of his squadmates, Tyko glanced at the score/time display. With less than twenty seconds remaining it would be difficult to work the quantam into position to score the six points needed to tie the match. They gave it their all, but the buzzer sounded just moments before Henrik's desperation throw bounced off the end-board.

The teams lined up to exchange handshakes and with eyes down Tyko numbly and briefly touched the hands thrust at him. He had no way of knowing which hand belonged to the girl, but walking to the locker room he glanced back and saw her surrounded by celebrating teammates.

To his surprise, she was staring at him.

T wo weeks after arriving at Operating Post Tango-5 on Neptec-2, Sergeant Siengha was set to lead half her platoon out on an ambush. Standing next to the combat transport as soldiers from First Squad milled around the landing pad, she noted with satisfaction the five newest troops in her command were part of the group. Their armor was still noticeably unmarred after two weeks of outpost duty — standing perimeter watches and work details for housekeeping and improving defenses — but soon enough that would change.

Siengha rubbed her eyes and leaned back against the transport. As soon as the platoon arrived at OP Tango-5 she and Lieutenant N'dele were ordered to the Tactical Operations Center for a mission orientation briefing while the troops were directed to a berthing compartment to stow their gear. Inside the Ops Center the Top Sergeant handed her a data pad with watch and meal rotations for her people, and daily personnel requirements for work details; as Papa Sierra she would ensure everyone was where they needed to be.

Each squad was given a tour of the outpost the day of arrival and stood a perimeter watch supervised by soldiers from other platoons. Then they were on their own. Siengha would have preferred more time to settle in, but Third Platoon was at Tango-5 to take the place of a unit decimated by a Vyp ambush and everyone else at the post had been pulling extra duty to cover the gap. She knew the experienced members of her platoon would get the most important information from the old-timers at the post, but worried about the five new soldiers.

Siengha believed it best to scrub the newness off green troops as soon as possible, and that meant going eye-to-eye with the enemy in the field — not standing a perimeter watch. At first these watches would be stressful for the newbies but as the days went by they would grow more comfortable with them and that could be their undoing outside the outpost's walls. She felt so strongly about getting them blooded, as it was called, that at the orientation briefing just minutes after arriving at Tango-5 she volunteered her platoon for the next patrol outside the walls.

Her offer was met by icy stares from the officers and senior non-coms surrounding the major in charge of the post (who had been the operations officer until the Vyps downed the transport carrying both the colonel in command and her executive officer). Ignoring the others, whose soldiers were standing extra watches, the major paused a moment before replying.

"I appreciate wanting to get your new people blooded, Sergeant Siengha. I'd do the same if I was in your position. But the priority for the post is getting your platoon into the rotation, so I've got to say no."

Siengha nodded and thanked the major, coming away from that first meeting with a positive impression of the officer whose decisions could well decide whether she lived or died at the outpost. He seemed tactically competent and a good leader, and she had seen more than her share of the other side of those qualities during the war. The junior officers and non-coms at Tango-5 were more of a mixed bag, but that was true everywhere.

On the landing pad, she felt a tap on her shoulder and turned her head just far enough to see a thumbs-up sign from a one of the aircrew. Nodding slightly, she pushed her shoulders and back off of the transport.

"LOAD UP!"

Although the same model as the ship that brought them to Tango-5, the transport was a combat variant which meant there were no seats. Long bars were attached to the deck and bulkheads to provide handholds, but otherwise the passenger compartment was empty. Siengha stood near the combat hatch and counted heads as the soldiers climbed in. The middle of the compartment quickly filled as the first men and women squatted or flopped down around the deck handholds, leaving those later in the queue to squeeze past or take spots near the large opening at the rear of the transport.

Siengha recognized the logic: in a contested landing the first and last out of the transport faced the greatest danger.

Her count complete, she tapped the aircrewman's shoulder and he toggled the switch to close the hatch. The sergeant noted without surprise the five replacement soldiers were clustered around her next to the exit. One by one, she began to check their equipment, pulling on straps and belts, and probing armor seals. The transport jumped up from the landing pad as she finished checking the second one, causing the green soldiers to hurriedly grab for handhold bars while Siengha easily shifted her weight to compensate for the movement. Grabbing the next soldier in line by the shoulder, she pulled the young man away from the bulkhead to check his load.

"S-sergeant." He swallowed hard and Siengha knew doing so left his throat sore as there wasn't much moisture to ease the passage. "I, uh, don't know if ... I mean, ah, I don't think I—"

She jabbed a finger into his face. "That's right, Haapala, don't think. Leave that to those of us who know what's going on. Just do what you're told."

"That goes for all of you," she added, turning to take in the whole group. "Remember your training, do what you're told. Keep your eyes and ears open. Follow orders. You'll be fine."

She went back to Haapala and continued her inspection. After pulling a carrypack strap to tighten it, she reached up and tapped the front of his helmet before moving to the next in line. Siengha knew the fear was burning in their guts; there was nothing anyone could say to make it go away. In a fight they would overcome the fear or they wouldn't. Either way, death or injury was a possibility.

For the next half-hour the transport executed a series of combat approaches at various locations, dipping into small valleys or behind hills to hover over the ground for seconds before jumping back up and roaring off. The terrain around the outpost was hilly and arid, with sparse ground vegetation and few trees.

The humans knew they were under constant surveillance by the Vyps, so deploying a ground force outside the perimeter required deception to prevent the soldiers from being overwhelmed shortly after touchdown. After Siengha's half-platoon was inserted the transport would continue simulating approaches for another twenty minutes before returning to the outpost.

Their landing was unopposed and the soldiers quickly formed up into a column and marched from the insert site. They changed directions twice before heading toward a small valley to the east of the outpost. Their objective was to set an ambush along a path suspected of being used by the Vyps to infiltrate observer teams near the post's perimeter.

Drones and high-alt reconnaissance showed the aliens used several routes to move their forces in and out — they, too, played the deception game — but the path Siengha and her group were targeting was deemed to have the highest amount of activity by the intelligence section at the outpost.

If the ambush was successful, Siengha was authorized to engage any alien observer teams she could locate near the perimeter. Otherwise, they were to fall back to an extract point for pick up by transport. Although they'd never been on this ground before, she and the squad leader developed the ambush plan using hi-res images and vid from drones. Before boarding the transports the squad gathered in the outpost mess hall where Siengha briefed the plan using the images, assigning each soldier a specific location and tasking.

At the ambush site, the squad split into three teams with Siengha leading a fire team to the spot designated as the kill zone. Her team quickly set up directional/remote detonation mines, called DRDs, in an L-shape to frame half of an imaginary rectangle over ground the Vyps were expected to traverse. Half the DRDs were angled so their shrapnel would fan out at four feet above ground level; the others were set to one foot. After placing the DRDs the team moved into positions among rocks at the base of two hills where the valley ended.

Led by Corporal Miroslav, the squad leader, the second group took an overwatch position fifty feet behind and slightly below the longest line of DRDs. Some hid among rock scree at the base of a hill and the rest dug shallow fighting positions in open ground. The squad's final fire team was placed in a support position on a small spur rising above the valley.

Once in place, the soldiers covered themselves with color-shiftable tarps, programmed at the outpost from the same pics used to plan the ambush, and settled in to wait.

Hours passed and the light faded as their location on Neptec-2 rotated away from the system's star. Siengha enabled the night vision feature on her faceshield and sipped from her water tube. Some of her soldiers had installed food tubes containing protein paste, but she was not much for eating before a fight. She flexed her limbs and neck frequently to maintain circulation and occasionally got on the platoon net to remind the others to do the same.

One of the lessons Command learned after the war's first battles was the need for two-way communication on tactical nets. Whenever one of her soldiers spoke or made a noise loud enough to activate the system the name appeared on Siengha's faceshield. It didn't surprise her in the least to see the five new replacements having the toughest time dealing with the wait. Haapala especially had trouble moderating his breathing, but eventually even he settled in.

* * * *

"Contact." She recognized the calm voice of Private First Class Sopheap, leader of the support fire team posted on the spur, without needing the digital display. More than six hours had passed since the ambush was put in place and it was the darkest point in the daily time cycle.

Ignoring the small noises made by the squad as they came to full readiness, Siengha studied the greenish outlines of twelve Vyptellian soldiers steadily moving toward her and the killzone. As she expected, the smaller aliens were to the front, with the largest of the dozen, at least a foot taller and likely their sergeant, about a third of the way from the rear. Command long ago realized Vyps continued to physically grow for at least a year after reaching military-service age, which meant at least half the group walking into the kill zone were likely inexperienced soldiers.

Siengha counted on this, which is why the DRD firing switch was in her hands. With their vast numbers and preference for mass assaults, she knew the aliens who survived and moved into command positions would put their greenest soldiers out front to absorb attacks. From long experience she knew the trick with ambushes was to have the nerve to wait until the most experienced Vyps would be cut down, even if it meant some aliens escaped initial harm.

After the DRDs fired, the fire team with her would move in to finish off any Vyps that survived the mine blasts or were outside the kill zone. They'd use blades to keep the noise down and ensure no friendly-fire incidents. Siengha placed her five new soldiers, the ones to be blooded, in this group.

As the first of the Vyp group entered the kill zone, several names popped up on Siengha's faceshield as members of the squad took in deep breaths. Some, like Haapala, appeared a second and third time as those soldiers struggled with their fright. In contrast, she was completely calm.

In the third year of the war Siengha served with an older sergeant whose favorite saying was: *What happens, happens.* When she questioned this philosophy his response was a wink and wintery smile. But one night, after a sharp fight, the sergeant began talking as the two of them shared a cup of tea.

"Always do everything you can to prepare, private. Always. Plan 'til your eyes cross, train 'til you drop, load the right gear in the right amount." She found herself nodding slowly as he continued, *"Find the right ground to fight on or if you can't then do your best to prepare the ground you got. Put your people in the right places with the right stuff, with the best plan you can come up with."*

Then the grizzled sergeant's voice grew softer and one corner of his mouth turned down. *"But know this: in the end, no matter how ready you are ... what happens, happens. Best prepared doesn't always win."*

The first three Vyps walked through the short line of DRDs facing them without noticing the mines. "Stand by," Siengha quietly said over the net as the last of the aliens entered the killzone.

At that moment the fourth Vyp in line suddenly stopped, its head clearly angled downward. The DRDs were small and hidden among the rocks and bushes, and Siengha was counting on the less experienced aliens at the front to not notice the deadly objects at their feet. But this one evidently had, and as the Vyp straightened and began to turn back toward its leader Siengha touched her finger to the control pad of the DRD firing switch.

Half the DRDs fired as one, filling the small valley with a sharp crackling noise and a flash of bluish light. Small hardened needles scythed through the Vyp formation at high speed, felling the aliens in the kill zone. Four seconds later the remaining DRDs fired, shredding low brush and supine Vyp bodies.

Four Vyps survived the blasts. The three that walked through the killzone before the mines fired had no time to react before the assault team with Siengha jumped out at them with swinging assault rifles and stabbing blades. The fourth Vyp, the one that discovered the hidden mines, had one leg amputated by the initial DRD blast and lived through the second only because its torso fell forward, out of the kill zone.

Siengha noted with satisfaction this alien was killed by Haapala.

The sergeant watched from her position among the rocks as the assault team examined the dead aliens. Not too many years earlier it had been her out there, rushing from cover to kill the enemy with her blade and then checking the bodies. She didn't miss that, exactly, but some days being Papa Sierra she longed for the simplicity of it.

Had she been a grunt, though, Siengha would have died with the assault team and most of the other soldiers in the squad when the kill zone switched sides.

There was almost no warning, just a sudden series of loud but strangely hollow metallic sounds which she knew came from Vyp projectiles. Calling out a warning on the net, Siengha threw herself to the rocky ground as the small valley filled with a bright greenish light that disrupted her night vision. She didn't look up — didn't need to and wouldn't even if there was time — as razor-sharp darts shredded any human flesh not shielded by rocks.

Later, after examining drone and surveillance vid, the intelligence types at the outpost would determine the Vyp sergeant had pre-registered a cannonade fire mission using its own position as the aim point. They were unsure if this indicated a new tactic and whether the alien survived the DRD blasts long enough to call in the cannonade or if the fire mission was automated, somehow tied into the Vyp's health status.

Rising unhurt from the rocks near the mouth of the valley, Siengha knew only this: she needed to collect any survivors and move out before the Vyps arrived.

What happens, happens.

Ribbons and Funerals

The old woman trudged up the hill to the mine office with her head down. Short and thick through the body, at sixty-seven she was in better shape than a few of the teenagers she supervised on the evening shift. Long gray hair pulled back into a high ponytail rhythmically slapped against her shoulders with each step.

As a girl she was considered quite attractive and the years living in the chilly, wind-swept mountains north of Xhialgong's upper-third meridian mellowed but did not completely erase the features that drew men and women to her.

She walked on the left side of the street, avoiding the deep shadows cast by rows of tall apartment buildings to her right. The sun was low in the sky that time of day and she savored the warmth on her face and hands. Glancing up at the buildings, she saw row upon row of dark windows. In each was a card with an orange triangle indicating a family member serving in the military; most windows displayed several triangles.

A familiar thought came to mind: *Even the few with no one in the war put up the orange to not stand out.*

In the earliest days people draped black ribbons on the triangles to indicate killed in action and blue ribbons for those wounded. Losses mounted and soon there were so many ribbons that people stopped doing it. Now without knowing someone personally it was hard to know exactly how much the war had cost them.

The woman and her husband gave all four of their children to the war. Just one came back, her eldest son. He lost two limbs and an eye but was still in the military, stationed at a recruit depot as an instructor. The war had also taken three of her grandchildren — all missing and presumed dead. Two more would soon be old enough to receive draft notices, and there were three more after that.

The woman would bear the future losses alone. Her husband died five years earlier, his heart stopped while he was on shift at the mine, five miles below the surface. He'd worked at the mine his whole life, was at least a decade away from mandatory retirement, and appeared to be in fine physical shape for a man in his mid-sixties.

By the time the settlement's octogenarian doctor made it to the mine her husband's co-workers had carried the body up to the front gate. Then they returned to the face to continue their shift. She didn't blame them for that: most were teenagers still too young for the military and had grown up inured to death and injury.

And there were quotas to meet.

After a year she stopped wondering if her husband would have lived had there been a doctor in the settlement not past his prime or at least on site at the mine that day. Or if there had been up-to-date medical supplies and equipment in the tunnels. The spark of anger she felt slowly died away. There was no point. The war had first priority on things like doctors, supplies, and equipment.

She left the shelter of the apartment blocks behind, lowering her head into the cold wind as she came to an open area just below the mine entrance. The settlement's schools were here, set back from the road. Two long, low buildings: one shared by primary and middle grades, and the other was the upper school. A handful of children, too young to have jobs, played on the three quantam courts between the schools and road.

The woman had attended classes in both buildings, graduating with a ceremony held in the upper school auditorium. She had never been away from the settlement for more than a few weeks through all her life and had never left the planet. At one time she wanted to travel, to roam the darkness of space like the people who left Old Earth on the Long Exodus. But that wasn't her fate.

She loved learning and became a teacher herself, spending nearly forty years working with the settlement's children. She started out and spent most of that time in the primary grades, and lived to see the spark of understanding in the young faces of her students.

But then there was the war and she was moved to the middle and upper grades to take the place of teachers called to the military.

The curriculum had changed greatly since her days as a student. Gone for the most part were the classics of Old Earth literature and media she remembered so fondly, replaced by lessons on military science or studies of Old Earth's wars.

The older students were different, too. They all worked jobs before or after school, most in the mine but also in shops and a small factory producing fuses used in smart munitions. So many older children were needed to fill vacant jobs that night school was started for those working day shifts.

In class, these kids were less interested in learning than catching up on their sleep and in time she stopped waking them. They needed their rest and soon enough the military would have them. In uniform, they'd learn all they needed to know about fighting and killing

She quit teaching after attending the remembrance ceremony for the last living student of the first middle school class she taught. It was one thing to realize an entire generation of the settlement was being wiped out, but it was too much to know each of them personally. The woman remembered when funerals were held, with bodies to be buried or cremated. In this war many died but there were no bodies, so the funeral rite became the remembrance ceremony.

Yet another example of the countless ways the war altered their lives.

Approaching the gated entrance to the mine, she studied the faces of the boys and girls waiting in line. She had been the primary grade teacher for many of them, and had taught some of their parents, too. It was depressing to know the future of these children was already set: working in the mine until they turned eighteen and then off to the war.

The woman watched as they pushed through the mine gate and headed off to work in the shafts. At their age, her future had been a mystery. She could do or be whatever she wanted. Old Earth's Utopian Ideal had been felt throughout the colony, even in her small settlement. Humanity had outgrown fighting over territory, religion, race, gender and sexual orientation.

Sadness momentarily overwhelmed her, and she put a hand on her chest until it passed. How could so much change in so few years? Could they ever go back to the way things once were?

The woman sighed and pushed her thoughts away as she passed through the gate. There was a long shift to be worked and quotas to be made. A sickness was going around and she expected to be short at least a few workers. Also, several ore processors were off-line for maintenance and she needed to check on the status of repairs.

There would be time enough later to worry about the future and miss the past.

Discoveries

"**W**hat did you do next?" The squadron support officer looked up from the notes on his datapad, eyebrows raised and head tilted slightly to one side.

Fighting the urge to roll his eyes, Tyko glanced at his hands, folded and resting on the table that separated him from the support officer. *We've been over this three times now*, he thought, *and by now you should have the vid of what happened.*

Tyko was annoyed when the patrol was terminated early, but that changed to unease when he and the three new pilots were escorted to debriefing rooms just off the flight deck. When he first got to the station, pilots were debriefed frequently and he had looked forward to having the chance to examine his actions and learn from his mistakes. Over time, the debriefs stopped, with no reason given.

Now, having finished going over the patrol for a second time, Tyko was back to being annoyed: There was nothing wrong with how he or the others performed, no reason for them to be pulled from the mission early. He suspected something else was going on.

Perhaps the support officers were reminding him they were keeping a close watch. Or, maybe they weren't satisfied with his reaction to being assigned to escort the wing's newest pilots on their first combat sortie.

Gaining and losing pilots was a continuous, but predictable, cycle. Squadrons rarely fell below full strength. With healthy and fit teenage pilots, far removed from actual combat, most vacancies resulted from illness or rec hall injuries. Very rarely, there were cases of pilots who demonstrated mental unsuitability for combat or military service.

By far the biggest source of turnover was age: when pilots turned eighteen they transferred from the station. Some retained their flight status, serving as staff officers, academy instructors, or transport pilots, but most opted to join the Expeditionary Forces — to become ground pounders and take the fight directly to the Vyptellians.

So getting new pilots blooded was a necessary task, but one usually given to much less capable and experienced pilots. It was a bit of a surprise to hear his name called at the flight cycle pre-brief, but Tyko assumed it was just another test to see if he'd learned his lesson from being suspended.

In his mind, he had.

As he had with all assignments since returning to flight status, Tyko accepted it without complaint. Before the patrol he pulled the three green pilots aside to answer their questions and tell them what to expect and how to react. He reminded them it was likely each would lose their fighter in the first few minutes of combat, but they shouldn't dwell on it.

After taking control of their fighters he took them through some flight and formation drills to assess their strengths and weaknesses before leading them into the engagement zone. Throughout, he followed all flight protocols to the letter, knowing the new pilots would be closely watching. He didn't want them starting out with any bad habits.

Suddenly aware of the silence in the room, Tyko looked up at the support officer and nodded. "After Xemal was hit I came about, crossed behind Schmiller. The Vyp didn't do what I expected and instead veered off to the right. I pursued, got into position and fired."

"That's the second time you mentioned the enemy was unpredictable. Why do you think that was?"

"They seemed new, like our pilots. The ones with me today, I mean." Tyko stifled a yawn and shifted in his seat. "I suppose they didn't know any better."

"You don't think they were trying new tactics?"

Tyko knew what he thought, but paused for a moment as if considering the question. "No. Like I said they didn't move like Vyps who've been in a fight before. You know, you should have the vid by now."

A ghost of a smile appeared on the support officer's face. "Regardless, we need to document your memories and opinions. What you saw, why you took the actions you did."

Tyko nodded and swallowed another yawn. He finished his account in a few more sentences. When he was done they sat in silence, the support officer looking over the notes on his datapad and Tyko glancing around the room.

It occurred to him then that they were waiting for something, or someone. That the reason he told the same story three times was to give time to prepare whoever or whatever was coming next.

Tyko looked down at his hands and wondered what was being served for dinner in the mess hall, and more importantly if Caviness would wait for him there. Probably not, he decided. She had been standing in a knot of pilots from other squadrons watching Henrik flight test the new interceptor when he climbed into his control unit for the patrol.

She gave him a quick smile as he strapped in, a smile he shyly returned.

Caviness was still there when he and the three new pilots were escorted to the debriefing rooms. He was sure she noticed how short their flight time had been but was probably too involved in observing the new fighter in action to give it much thought.

After Henrik's flight she may have waited for him on the flight deck. Perhaps she went to the mess hall to sit at the table in the corner where she had introduced herself to him a week earlier (and where they had eaten every meal together since). Or maybe she just left, walking past the door to the debriefing room he was in on her way back to her own squadron in Third Wing.

Tyko's shoulders slumped a little at the thought of not being able to see her again until breakfast.

She had been on his mind a lot in the days after his squadron's loss in the quantam semi-final — the girl with the bright blue eyes and sideways smile. Tyko found himself scanning the faces of other pilots in the rec hall and library, or any time he left Fourth Wing's section of the station. He knew the odds of finding her were long.

She was part of Third Wing but so were more than a thousand other pilots. At some point the math would work out, his squadron and hers would be on the same rotation, but without knowing her name or squadron all he could do was study passing faces.

Then one day he was eating breakfast and heard a small cough at his shoulder. Looking up from a steaming bowl of grain cereal he saw those eyes and that smile. Tyko stammered a greeting and invited her to join him.

"Morning. I'm Caviness," she said, placing her tray on the table across from him.

"I'm Tyko." His face felt warm and he forced himself to look down at his cereal, worried his staring would unnerve her.

"I know." She smiled and raised a spoonful of cereal to her mouth. Caviness blew on the spoon before continuing. "I'm on temp assignment to learn about the Mark 6 from you."

"Oh." Tyko sighed and looked away, his cheeks growing hotter. "That's not me. You'll be working with Henrik. He's very good, great even. You'll learn a lot."

The smile disappeared from her face and her eyelids narrowed. They ate in silence for a bit before she set her spoon down and quietly asked the question he wanted her not to ask.

Without a thought of lying or evading, Tyko told her about walking into Pri-Fly and his suspension, giving her the few details he was allowed to tell. He was surprised the story hadn't spread to her wing but then she told him it had, just with no name attached.

They finished their breakfast in silence and then she chuckled. "Hey. We lost the station championship."

"I know ... to a squad from First Wing. I would've gone to watch but I was on duty."

"That makes sense." Her eyes crinkled. "I looked for you, in the crowd."

"Oh?"

Caviness giggled a little. "Yes. I thought you'd want to see if the team that beat yours won the title."

"Hmm."

"Also to see if you were a sore loser."

"And since I didn't show, you thought I was?" Tyko laughed when she shrugged and looked away. "No, you beat us fair. Those last points, you were quicker."

"Thanks."

From that point on they ate every meal together, Caviness joining him even when the other pilots on temp assignment returned to their own squadrons. For the first time in his years of Fleet service Tyko found himself looking forward to something other than flying and battling Vyps. During patrols he counted the minutes to turnover so he could join her at the table in the corner of the mess hall.

The door to the debriefing room opened, snapping Tyko back to the present as the support officer jumped to his feet. Assuming a senior officer had entered the room, Tyko followed suit, painfully hitting his thighs on the table in the process. He stood at attention, looking directly ahead until his squadron commander and an officer he didn't recognize came into view.

"That'll be all, lieutenant. Thank you," the commander said with a nod, prompting the support officer to quickly exit. Her next words, spoken before the door closed, made Tyko forget about Caviness and dinner. "Flight Officer Tyko, this is Major Tham, the Air Group intelligence officer."

Tham was older, in his late forties by Tyko's estimate, with a narrow face and close-set eyes under bushy eyebrows. If Tyko's heart sank at the sight of his squadron commander taking over the debriefing, it stopped beating with Tham's presence. The young pilot's daily life revolved around his squadron; he rarely had any dealings with the air wing and to his knowledge had never been in the same room as an officer from the Air Group in charge of the station's flight operations.

Tyko swallowed with some difficulty and nodded at the major. His squadron commander and Tham pulled out chairs and sat down, leaving Tyko standing on legs that felt rubbery. After a moment the commander nodded and gestured for him to sit down.

"Thank you, ma'am."

"Tyko, the major and I just watched the patrol vid from your fighter, but we'd like to hear from you what happened." The commander sat back and considered him with unblinking eyes. "Start from the initial engagement with the enemy."

He told them how the four-ship group entered the outer edge of the engagement zone, Tyko leading the way followed by Schmiller, Coldron and Kemal. He scanned ahead, looking for a good spot to throw the new pilots into the fray when a flight of six Vyps came at them from their left. It was surprising, but not unprecedented. Vyps usually preferred straight-on attacks, relying on sheer numbers to overcome their enemy's greater skill and equipment.

He ordered the others to make a hard diving turn to the left, increase throttles to full power and engage the enemy. Tyko's plan gave the new pilots the best chance of surviving long enough to send some charged slugs in the direction of the enemy — as he saw it, a reasonable outcome given their lack of experience. At the same time, he would turn but remain level with the oncoming Vyps, drawing their fire while engaging from a low-percentage angle.

Tyko ignored the excited yelps and cries from the others and focused on his own ship and fight. After coming around, the targeting reticle briefly flashed twice as his fighter's nose passed the oncoming Vyp formation. He fired blindly, sending out streams of green while hoping to give the new pilots time to move into better positions. Some of his slugs found their target: a bright flash of light in the darkness of space ahead was followed moments later by another.

Then he was past the line of Vyp fighters and using the flight controls and throttle to twist his own ship into a series of tight turns. Tyko expected to hear a warning warble indicating at least one of the Vyp fighters had locked on to his fighter, but instead his earphones filled with the excited chatter of his patrol mates as they engaged the enemy.

He concluded that the Vyps were also new, and decided to let the two groups of green pilots flail at each other while monitoring his displays for new threats. When Coldron's fighter exploded, Tyko pushed his throttle forward and headed back toward the battle, slowing down after a few seconds as he came across a motionless Vyp fighter. The enemy ship was nearly intact, split in half near the cockpit, which was something of a rarity: enemy ships usually fragmented into thousands of pieces.

This is one of the strangest patrols I've ever been on, Tyko thought with a wry grin. *Can't wait to tell Caviness about it.*

Then one of the Vyps blew up Kemal's ship and Tyko decided it was time to end the lesson. Pushing his throttle to full, he acrobatically moved through the swirling Vyps, destroying three of the remaining five enemy ships with as many bursts of fire. The final two Vyps fled at full speed and Tyko ordered Schmiller to form up on him.

He set a course for the rally point where replacement fighters would be waiting for Kemal and Coldron, and requested Schmiller's fuel and ammo status. Before she could reply a flight controller came on the net, ordering them to depart the engagement zone and await relief.

"A few minutes after that we turned the ships over and were escorted here." Tyko sat back in his chair and folded his hands in his lap. He looked expectantly at the major and squadron commander, waiting for their questions.

"The enemy ship you went past, you mentioned it was unusual to see a destroyed Vyp fighter." Tham's eyes were locked on Tyko's. "How rare would you say it was?"

"Very. In over two years I've seen two others. Neither was as ... whole, I guess you'd say, as the one today. Much smaller pieces but still you could see what it was ... had been."

"That was a concise, but very complete report, Flight Officer Tyko," Tham said with a nod. "Any final impressions, last thoughts about what happened, what you may have seen?"

Although he didn't have to think about it, couldn't imagine what more they thought he knew, Tyko paused a moment before shaking his head. "No, sir."

"Thank you. You're to say nothing of this debriefing or what happened on the patrol to anyone without permission from myself or your squadron commander. I'm told you're quite familiar with the consequences of disobeying orders, so I trust you'll follow my orders."

Tham got to his feet and shuffled past the squadron commander and out of Tyko's sight. There was a slight pause before the door opened and he saw his squadron commander nod, then the door closed. Tyko turned his head, half expecting to see Tham standing behind him, but they were alone in the debriefing room.

The squadron commander leaned forward and spoke, her voice low. "You've earned back some of my trust, Tyko, so I'm going to share a bit more with you. Based on analysis of the vid, the Vyp fighter you flew past was the first one you hit. It appears your slugs hit at the perfect angle to crack open the airframe without causing a fatal explosion."

"It was a lucky shot, ma'am. I couldn't do that again if I tried."

"I expect not, but that's not really the interesting part." The commander leaned back and rubbed a hand across her face. "First, those Vyps were not new pilots. In fact, intelligence believes they were probably among their most experienced."

Tyko felt sudden confusion as he scanned his memory for clues he may have missed. Nothing about what the commander said made sense based on what he saw. His face betrayed his thoughts because her lips curled into a wry smile.

"You didn't miss anything, Tyko. You just weren't looking for it." The smile disappeared. "One of the flight controllers noticed it, actually. You cut the Vyp fighter in half at just the right spot, and then we enhanced the vid, studied it millisecond by millisecond to confirm."

"Ma'am? I'm sorry but ... confirm what?"

"There was no Vyp inside. They're experimenting with remote piloting."

A SINGLE STEP

R his stared at the document on his datascreen. The Hrustians were uncharacteristically delaying approval of several contracts and he was trying to figure out why.

Hearing a small stir from the desks around him, Rhis looked up to see a soldier walk into the office. The woman was mid-twenties, wearing smart-looking dress blues that displayed her athletic build but didn't hide a missing arm.

Must be waiting to be fitted for a prosthetic, Rhis thought. Or, perhaps she was one of the ones deciding to live without an artificial limb. Along with many of his co-workers at the Diplomatic Ministry he'd seen a recent news vid about this emerging trend among returning soldiers, and there was a lively discussion about the meaning behind it.

Rhis pretended to read while watching the soldier. She stopped at his section head's desk and after a short conversation both turned to look at him. Rhis felt a wave of uncertainty pass through him. *Surely they can't need people like me to fight now?*

He was nearly fifty-five, with the pale complexion and flabby body of an office drone whose time was spent either at home or work. As a teenager, Rhis played quantam and dreamed of doing something creative, like writing or painting. He only accepted an internship at the Diplomatic Ministry as a way to finance the pursuit of that goal. The work was dreary but the income and prestige of a career diplomat convinced him to forget about the arts. He opted for government service upon reaching the age of majority and studied economic theory at the Diplomatic University.

After graduating he was assigned to the Hrustian section where his responsibilities steadily increased — famously accepting of all, the commerce-minded aliens seemed to especially enjoy dealing with him — to the point where after the war started he was deemed too valuable for transfer to the military.

His commitment partner, however, was not. In his mid-thirties when the war began, Djovic was omitted from the first call-ups but in the third year of fighting an e-note arrived ordering him to report for military service. Despite all the upbeat reports from the Information Ministry, Rhis thought it a telling sign that someone his partner's age was needed for a war they were 'winning.'

They had been talking of adopting a child. It was Djovik's idea, actually, but Rhis listened. There were children in need of homes, many orphaned by the war. Rhis wasn't interested in children or family, but he was inclined to go along to make his partner happy. Then the draft notice arrived and Rhis turned against the adoption, claiming he was too old to be a single parent and his position at the ministry demanded too much of his time.

This reversal wounded Djovic greatly: he wanted a family to return to when the war was over. He tried to convince Rhis to reconsider the adoption, right up to the day his unit left New Earth. As Rhis feared, that was the last time he saw his partner: Djovic was reported 'Missing, Presumed Dead' a few months later.

Now more than ten years later, Rhis spent most of his days poring over the dreary details of inter-species business documents and all of his evenings cataloging his regrets. He'd always been circumspect, guarded, but after Djovic received the draft notice that innate introspection became a deep-seated pessimism.

Occasionally, he was required to travel from New Earth to Hrus on diplomatic missions. The Hrustians he dealt with, business owners and mid-level members of government, were universal in their disbelief the humans would attempt a war against the Vyptellians.

"Despite all warning from Hrus, you have fallen into conflict with the Vyptellians. Such an unwise choice," said one of his counterparts, KB-11356 (disconcerting at first, humans came to accept Hrustian naming conventions).

This exchange, which happened about a year after Djovic's death, prompted him to think about the war in ways he previously hadn't. Like everyone he knew, Rhis was appalled and angered by the sudden attack on the settlers of Nex Altrien. Calls for 'justice for those murdered' were heard from every part of the colony, including the Representative Legislature. Rumors and fear ran through the population like plague and soon many were convinced the aliens planned to exterminate humanity.

The Council responded to the popular outcry by empowering the Military Command to take all necessary measures to ensure the safety of New Earth and its population. Sixteen bloody years of war later, the war was a shadow over every part of life and Nex Altrien was rarely thought of or mentioned.

Rhis said nothing either way, but secretly he wondered if those with the loudest voices would still scream for justice if they knew what it would lead to. Military equipment and supplies were the first priority of most industries, and there was no funding for scientific research without an obvious wartime application. Further limiting the expansion of human knowledge, exploration of the galaxy was considered too dangerous.

And, of course, there were the tens of thousands killed and injured. Few household were untouched by this most direct result of the war.

Now with his heart pounding, Rhis watched the soldier curtly nod to the supervisor and walk toward his desk. He gave up the pretense of reading and sat back in his chair, his hands folded and resting on his stomach. The one-armed soldier stopped in front of the desk and looked down at him.

"Your presence has been requested at a meeting elsewhere in the ministry. I am to escort you."

"What? What meeting is this? I'm afraid no one informed me of any —"

"I'm informing you right now. If you would follow me ... sir." She had the pained look of a highly trained professional dealing with a matter wholly beneath her station.

Rhis smiled without meaning to, before getting to his feet and following her toward the door. He glanced at his supervisor but she had her head down and seemed to be engrossed in something on her display. *Pretenses everywhere today*, he thought with a bitterness that was surprising and shameful.

Walking at a brisk pace as if to keep Rhis behind her, the soldier led him to the section of the building where the liaison offices of Military Command were located. They paused in the reception area just long enough for him to be issued a visitor pass — he pressed his thumb to a touchscreen attached to the wall and a small yellow card emerged from a slot beneath — and then she led him into a well-lit corridor lined with closed doors.

No open plan offices for the military, he thought idly. His escort stopped at a door guarded by two armed soldiers wearing armor. Without a word to Rhis or the guards, she pushed the door open and gestured for the diplomat to enter.

The office was nearly as large as the one he shared with the twenty people in his section. A large desk was at the end farthest from the door, but it was the long conference table — and the man and woman seated at the table — that drew his attention. The man was one of the Diplomatic Ministry's three vice-ministers and the woman was a four-garland general and deputy of Military Command.

Rhis had exchanged banal pleasantries with the minster at countless functions during his career, and the general's grim visage seemed to be a mandatory part of most news vids dealing with the war. The two-garland general who served as liaison between the two ministries was absent — lending his office for this meeting was evidently his sole contribution.

The door closed behind him and Rhis leaned back against it, his head suddenly light. This caused the general to shake her head with a smirk but the vice-minister jumped to his feet and approached Rhis.

"Come, come, Rhis. Join us, please. We have something very important to discuss with you." The man took Rhis by the arm and led him to the table. Looking down at the minister, Rhis noted that his visitor badge was gold. *Different depending on security clearance* passed through his mind as he sank into the chair the other man pulled out for him.

"Important, to discuss with me?" Rhis looked up at the vice-minister, who remained standing behind him. A sudden thought crashed into his mind, and his voice quavered a bit: "Is this, ah, about the problems we're having with the Hrustians?"

The minister smiled and shook his head. "No, no, this has nothing to do with the Hrustians. I'm sure we'll have those issues sorted in short order." He pulled out the chair next to Rhis and sat down. "I suppose it makes sense you would think that's why we wanted to talk to you."

The general leaned forward and locked eyes with Rhis. "We have a mission for you, a mission more important than anything you've ever done before."

"Mission?" Rhis looked at the minister, confusion on his face. "I'm a diplomat, not a soldier. I don't … I'm not … *trained*, for missions … in the military sense."

"Consider it a tasking, then. The terms are really

interchangeable." The minister's smile didn't fade, but also didn't quite extend to his eyes. "There is something of vital importance to the future of humanity, and we need you to do it."

"Me?" Rhis said it with a shaky laugh: it seemed a terribly absurd statement. "What could you possibly need me to do that would be vitally important to humanity?"

"The Council has appointed you as a peace emissary." The general didn't blink — never seemed to blink — and her voice was measured, without emotion. "You will travel to the Talet system for orientation and final preparations, and from there on to where it is our hope you will make contact with the Vyptellians."

Oblivious to his gaped mouth, the general continued providing details that Rhis only half-heard: Immersion training on Vyptellian customs, specially developed translation software, an unarmed ship sent into enemy-controlled space while broadcasting a request for parley.

"Wait ... wait." Rhis took a deep breath, shook his head. "I'm not sure I understand any of this. You want me to make contact with the Vyptellians?"

Anger flashed across the general's face but before she could say anything the vice-minister spoke up. "Yes. We, the Council and Military Command, are asking you ... do you recall Old Earth's ancient history? Wars between cities or nations, not species? As they did then, we are asking you to cross the battle line under a banner of peace."

"But to what end? Am I ... offering surrender?"

"Absolutely not!" The general's hand slapped down on the table with a crack. "You will have no authority to discuss any matters relating to the war. Your role is simply to make a connection ... to open a door."

"That's a good analogy." The minister's smile never wavered. "We want you to open the door. If ... when you are successful we anticipate that connection, the one you make, will lead to detailed discussions on a wide range of topics."

"Including an end to the war?" Rhis looked from the minister to the general.

"Ultimately. That is our hope," the vice-minister replied smoothly. "In many respects it will be no different than your dealings with the Hrustians. You don't originate the business ventures, merely facilitate them. As was said on Old Earth, every journey begins with a single step."

Rhis nodded, attempting to settle the swirl of thoughts and emotions running through his head. After a few moments of silence (welcomed by him, tolerated by the others) an idea took form. Perhaps this was a chance, *the* chance, to do something that would silence his regrets ... something big enough to erase every missed opportunity.

He looked sideways at the vice-minister, then across to the general. "I have two questions."

"Yes, of course."

"First: why now? I recall rumors of a delegation to Vyptellia shortly after the war's start, but nothing since."

"An excellent question, which I believe the general is best suited to answer. But first," the minister said, placing a hand on Rhis's forearm. "It is unwise to speculate on certain topics or repeat rumors, as I'm sure you know. This will be a unique undertaking: a first of historic importance. Now, general?"

The officer's lower face re-twisted into a smirk, but she spoke with the same level voice as before. "The war is not going poorly, if that's what you're implying. Rather the opposite. We've detected, and I must caution you that what I'm about to say is highly classified, well above your level —"

"I believe his clearance has already been updated." The minister dryly laughed.

"Yes, well. In several key sectors we've detected signs the Vyptellians are pulling back, or preparing to pull back their forces. Their tactics have changed in these key sectors as well, and these changes have been interpreted as being very favorable to us." The general cast a sideways glance at the minister. "Some believe they may even have come to the conclusion that victory is not possible. At any rate, Command believes a mission such as this, or a tasking — whatever the hell you want to call it — must come from a position of strength. Vyps understand strength."

"I see." Rhis nodded. His unease and surprise were fading quicker than he would have expected. "My second question is this: why me?"

"... Besides your long years of exceptional and loyal service?" The minster smiled his phony smile. "Several reasons — the most important being your connection to the Hrustians, and how they feel about you."

"We know they have maintained strict neutrality," the general added. "But we also know they communicate with the

Vyps and we expect anything they know about us, or in this case you, the Vyps will also know."

"And they know, and more importantly, trust you."

"I see." Rhis nodded again. "If this is something we have never tried before, we don't know how the Vyptellians will respond. They may destroy the ship no matter what message is being broadcast."

"Yes, that's true." The general's candor actually surprised Rhis.

He sighed and a memory of Djovic popped into his head, their final conversation. It was the morning his division shipped out. They'd had a big meal the night before, all of Djovic's favorites, and too much wine. Laying in bed before the sun came up, their bodies entwined, Djovic admitted to being afraid, but that he believed the war was just and worthy of their sacrifices.

Then and now, Rhis thought neither was true, but the bittersweet memory helped him ignore his fears.

"When do I leave?"

MOVEMENT

The observation deck was nearly full when Tyko got there. He stood at the back of the crowd next to a ladder leading up to Third Wing's deck and scanned the backs of heads, looking for Caviness. She was coming off patrol and he was going on, choosing to skip breakfast to see her in person for the first time in a month-and-a-half.

He took a break from searching for her to look at the large viewscreen mounted on the bulkhead at the far end of the compartment. It showed the blackness of space but Tyko recognized the star clusters twinkling in the distance: they were the same ones he always saw heading out to fight the Vyps. Two large, ungainly ships hovered in the middle distance, half of the Fleet of auxiliary craft that would tow the base station to a new position closer to the enemy.

The move was necessary because a month earlier the Vyptellians began pulling their forces back, forcing Tyko and the other pilots in the Air Group to fly farther from the station to engage them in battle. At the same time as the pull-back, the number of Vyp ships encountered began to decrease and those enemy fighters they did find seemed to be flown by very inexperienced pilots.

Rumors began circulating almost immediately, growing more and more outlandish as the days passed. One, told to Tyko and Caviness in the rec hall by a wide-eyed pilot from First Wing, was that a mysterious disease was sweeping through Vyp ranks, killing so many aliens they had no choice but to retreat. Lowering his voice to a conspiratorial whisper, the pilot added the disease was a bio-weapon perfected in a military-controlled lab on Xhialgong.

Tyko and Caviness laughed about this conversation later, sure that even if Command was desperate enough to try such a weapon the last person to uncover such highly classified information would be a teenage pilot on a front-line base station. But when the first whispers about Vyps converting to remotely piloted ships reached his ears, Tyko made an appointment with his squadron commander to assure her he hadn't said a word. To his relief, she nodded and told him she knew he hadn't. An officer in one of the other air wings was to blame.

In time, Fleet command revealed the Vyp remote piloting experiment as part of the order directing the line of base stations to move deeper into territory previously considered to be enemy-held. Tyko's part in uncovering this new intelligence was not mentioned by Fleet but the Air Group commander added it in a post script, creating a stir throughout the station.

His squadron mates, including the three pilots on the patrol with him, were shocked that Tyko knew such a large secret but hadn't said anything. Henrik shook his head and wondered aloud what other information he was keeping from them, drawing in response a sheepish grin from Tyko.

He was more worried about what Caviness would think. He felt a vague uneasiness about keeping the secret from her, but wasn't sure why — which in turn created more anxious feelings. But her nightly e-note was filled with congratulations and excitement at the role he played, and like everyone else she wondered if there was a larger purpose behind what the Vyps were doing.

In his reply note he confessed to being afraid she would be upset with him, but in her next message she wrote she understood and trusted him, and the euphoria he felt reading that lasted from breakfast until lights out.

That was yesterday. Now, as Tyko watched, one of the auxiliary ships suddenly began pulling away from the station — a move accompanied by a sudden rise in the noise level on the observation deck. He looked around again, searching for Caviness, and felt a sudden pang of nervousness at the thought of seeing her again.

As her temporary duty assignment with his squadron drew to a close, Tyko realized how much he would miss her. He wanted to tell her that and to ask about keeping in touch, but never got the chance. Two days before she was to return to her own squadron, Tyko learned that she had been recalled early because a member of her squadron had been slightly injured in the rec hall.

The deep depression he felt — Tyko barely remembered the pre-flight briefing, the patrol itself, or walking from the flight deck to his quarters — disappeared when he found an e-note from her in his message queue. That first message was just a few sentences, written before heading off on patrol. It was to tell him why she left, but it lifted his spirits to know she wanted him to understand what had happened. They wrote each other at least once a day after that and whenever Tyko entered his cabin he automatically looked at the net terminal, hoping to see the blinking green light indicating a new message.

Their schedules kept them apart so they filled their e-notes with daily activities: what they ate, how their patrols went, what they read or what vids they watched, and what they did in the rec hall. In no time (Tyko was surprised at how quickly, yet subtly, the shift occurred) they were sharing information about their families and hometowns, their goals, and even what they thought about the war.

Tyko was initially concerned about this development, knowing how everything they did was monitored by support officers, but neither of them wrote anything that wasn't openly discussed in ready rooms and mess halls. Mostly, they wondered how much longer it would take to defeat the Vyps.

The second auxiliary ship began to move, drawing Tyko's attention from the crowd. As the gray craft grew smaller on the viewscreen, he felt someone brush against his arm and then a small, sweaty hand slipped into his, interlacing fingers. He turned with a smile, his breath catching at the sight of her. Caviness's face was flushed after running from the Third Wing flight deck. She mouthed "Morning" and matched his smile, leaning into him until they were touching from her shoulder against his upper arm to their hips.

Somewhere in Tyko's mind a small voice told him their time was limited, but everything he had wanted to say evaporated from his thoughts. All he could do was look into her eyes. Instinctively, he leaned in and a wave of panic swept through him as her eyelids narrowed. He paused, worried about her reaction, but then her eyes closed and she tilted her chin up.

Their lips met and in that moment there was nothing else in the universe but the two of them.

WAR STORIES

U ncle: Greetings from the Talneptine system. I'm sure you're surprised to receive this note outside normal channels, but when I heard about a back-channel to send notes home (I suspect run by Fleet airmen), I decided to give it a try. I'm sending this to you and not my parents for reasons I'm sure will be obvious.

When I enlisted (What...ten months ago now? Seems so much longer!) you didn't argue against it like they did. I don't think you liked the idea, but you respected my decision. I know they were just scared of what may happen to me. I see from their notes that hasn't changed. I just couldn't live my life not knowing whether I was able to do this or not.

Things are strangely quiet here and if the rumors are to be believed, everywhere else, too. Are they telling you that back home? I bet they are. I'm sure they're saying at long last we have turned a corner, have the Vyps on the run, the end is near, etc. That's what they're telling us, at any rate. Maybe it's true, too. I don't know — I'm just a foot soldier and we're not paid to think.

But that's exactly the problem, Uncle. I can't stop thinking right now.

Command learned a lot about taking care of combat soldiers the past sixteen years. We rotate in and out of the battlezone regularly. Where I am now (about a half-hour from the battlezone by transport) has hot food & water, portable vid devices, and even a makeshift quantam court. The daily routine is light on duty so mostly I've slept, but I'm still new to this. The ones who've been out here the longest seem to have the least need for sleep. They're up all hours watching vids, reading or playing quantam.

In the field there isn't time to think: I'm hyper-alert all the time. Talneptine is quiet now, but just a few months ago (before I got here) there were battles lasting weeks. Now we patrol and look for Vyps, and they do the same. Sometimes we find each other and then we try to kill each other.

The Vyps have hunter/killer drones just like us, their cannon shoot as far as ours, and their shells are as powerful. They attack at night as much as during the day, which is to say any time they want. I've been taught how to kill them, and I have. I think that's the first question you'd have for me (but may not know how to ask). It would be my first question, too.

I killed two Vyps less than a day after getting here — one with my rifle , the other with my knife. There was no way not to, really. Out here we're like two wild animals thrown into a cage and only one can survive. I should not be surprised, or amazed by that — what else is war, really?

Still, it is jarring to see a soldier reading, or tossing a quantam around, and to remember him using a rifle to club a wounded Vyp to death just days or even hours earlier. We don't take prisoners, but we do leave the bodies of their dead — or what's left — for them to find. Sometimes we place hidden explosives on the corpses, but not every time — no sense getting predictable.

There is no time in the battlezone but back here I wonder about these small insults: if they serve a purpose or are just us expressing our anger and fear. I don't know if Vyps have emotions, but if they do they don't seem to respond to our provocations. Of course, they don't leave bodies behind to plant bombs on, or to show us for certain that our wounded have been brutalized and murdered, so how can we know?

How long would they lock me up, do you think, if I wondered aloud if there isn't a chance that humans and Vyps are related species? Surely Command has conducted tests on prisoners and knows for sure. If so, what does it say about our evolution if the lizards are the higher form?

Don't worry, I'm not going soft on the Vyps. How could I? They're trying every day to kill me, and may yet succeed. But they aren't the only ones trying.

Time to get to the point, I suppose. Here's a quick war story for you, Uncle — the war story that won't leave me alone.

A squad from another platoon in my company was assigned to break the trail for our movement from one location to another. It's dangerous, so going first — on point — gets rotated between platoons, and within platoons between the squads, and within squads between fire teams; sooner or later everyone gets the chance.

This squad left the perimeter at first light and we followed a couple hours later. After tramping along a rocky trail for some time we came up a small rise and found an injured soldier sitting with her back to a small dirt mound. Her head was leaning forward and one of her arms was off at the shoulder, a spot where the tourniquet feature of our armor isn't very effective. She also had wounds to both legs and one hip, but the arm was the most serious.

Blood was everywhere (something else you learn: there is so much more blood in even the smallest human than you realize until seeing it spread out) and my lieutenant immediately dispatched a fire team to follow the red trail marking her path. We only realized she was still alive when her head slowly came up. I saw her face through the shield and her eyes looked unfocused, unsure. The lieutenant put a hand on her uninjured shoulder and asked what happened, but she died without saying a word.

She was the first dead human I ever saw.

The officer called in her position and we got moving again. A little bit after that the fire team comm'd to say they'd found the rest of the squad about a klick ahead. There were no survivors; they were torn up pretty good. I think the woman we found must have been at the rear of the formation when the cannon shells, or whatever it was, hit them.

We marked it down as the Vyps, probably using drones to locate the squad. Everyone was on edge for the rest of the movement, but nothing else happened. I didn't think about the dead soldier and her squad again until we rotated back off the line.

I haven't stopped thinking about them since it came to me while I was eating my first hot food in a week.

It couldn't have been the Vyps, Uncle. They don't leave bodies behind if they have the time, and they had at least an hour (the blood was mostly dry). True, there may not have been a Vyp unit nearby but that isn't how they operate: their drones provide direct support and don't roam free over the battlezone.

Our drones do, though.

I want to believe we didn't kill that squad, but I think we did.

We have good officers in this company and I know they pre-register moves with cannon batteries and ask for drone overwatch. What would happen if the battery or drone controller loses that information? Without optics and network links, from a distance I'd be hard pressed to tell the difference between a human soldier and a Vyp standing side-by side. The coloration of armor is the biggest difference, but what if the drone vid processor shorted out and relayed low-def or even grayscale? Or if the soldier monitoring the drone's vid feed was tired?

For whatever reason, a mission was activated and explosive projectiles flew out and chewed up a squad of our soldiers.

I accept that mistakes happen, and here the consequences are severe. Forget to load your rifle? Don't seal your armor? Don't sweep for mines? Do these and you'll likely die. But are there consequences of the consequences?

The chain of command on-planet must realize what really happened, right? Of all people, the newest guy in the platoon can't be the only one to see it for what it is. So, somewhere on this rock are other people who know it was us who killed that squad, and even with the little I know about the military that means there are people off-planet who also know. How far up does the lie go? All the way back to New Earth?

I'm sure the families of the dead soldiers will never know and there will be no public reports from the Information Ministry. It can't matter to the soldiers who died, right? Dead is dead. They went away to a war that started when they were in primary school, and they died. Even if there wasn't a war, some of them would be dead no matter what. An accident, getting sick, a murder or even suicide. But there is a war, and a lot of people die in war, and in a lot of ways.

So why can't I stop thinking about this squad of people I didn't really know? Why do I wonder what their lives would have been like had there been no war or had they lived to see peace return?

And why did I lie to you before, about sleeping a lot? I suppose I needed to work up to telling you I need the small green pills in the med packs we're offered when we get to the rest area.

Right now, if you're still reading (and I think you are), you're wondering about sharing this with my father, at least, or maybe both of them. You know as much as anyone how fortunate I was to have such a close family growing up (as you suggested, I've indeed seen a wide range of situations among my fellow soldiers). My parents are good and simple people. If I hadn't enlisted, I know father would have spent whatever was necessary to expand his cultivation plot to keep me exempt from military service.

I leave it to you to decide what to tell them. If nothing else, pass along my love to them. Perhaps the war really is nearly won and my return is closer than I think. But that's just a hope, and I don't have much time for wishful thinking. We return to the battlezone in just a few hours.

COMMITMENT

Tyko fidgeted, his feet making small sounds against the colonel's rug, before leaning back against the cushions on the settee. He turned and looked to his left at the senior officer, who was sitting comfortably with legs crossed and one arm resting on the armrest. *Why am I missing a patrol?* Tyko thought.

"Tell me, Flight Officer Tyko. Do you hate the Vyptellians?"

The question was wholly unexpected. He sat up, dumbly staring at the Air Group support officer, the man every support officer on the station reported to. Was it a trick, another test of his loyalty? Would he ever be good enough again to erase that mistake?

Quickly his mind searched back through the eight months since his probation, looking for any potential wrong he may have committed.

"Well, do you?" The colonel's lips slowly flattened into a thin smile.

"They're our enemy. We're at war."

"That is the truth, but not an answer. We've been at war with the Vyps for your entire life, and war is hate on a grand scale." The senior officer leaned forward, his eyes locked on Tyko's. "Don't you think you should hate them?"

Slowly sinking back into the cushion, Tyko pondered the question. He grew up never knowing a time when humans weren't at war with the Vyptellians. Had he ever stopped to wonder what not being at war would be like?

Tyko couldn't remember if so.

Entire vid channels were dedicated to the conflict, with updates on battles and casualties. Heroes — usually killed in battle — were identified and glorified, extolled to the point where every schoolchild knew their name and what they'd accomplished fighting against an enemy always depicted as cruel and ruthless. In every vid Tyko ever saw, all the net-wide games he and his friends played, the Vyps were the bad guy — the ones they played *against*.

Did he hate the Vyps? They were targets to be destroyed, yes ... but did he hate them?

Hate was an emotion Tyko did not have much experience with. He knew from reading that hate was extremely negative, often visceral — a feeling of darkness about something or someone. He got along well with nearly everyone, and while he considered few to be his friends he had negative feelings about no one.

He was angry after being suspended, but the feeling didn't last and it wasn't directed at any one person. Tyko didn't think it could be considered hate.

Shouldn't he hate the Vyps, though? They were the enemy of his species, but no one he personally knew had ever been killed by a Vyptellian. Tyko thought back to Pri-Fly, and the horribly injured men and women there, but even that didn't stir dark thoughts in him. Those officers were the voices in his headset but he didn't know their names or anything about them.

"I should, but I don't." He said it so quietly at first he thought the colonel didn't hear. But then the older man leaned back and nodded.

"I'm not surprised. It wasn't a trick question, or a trap. I was just curious. You're barely teenagers when you get here, and the way you fight, through a screen ..."

The colonel suddenly leaned forward and grabbed an image frame from his desk. He turned it so Tyko could see there were two images inside, both of soldiers in the Expeditionary Forces. One was a male officer who looked to be in his mid-twenties and the other an enlisted female not much older than Tyko.

"These are my children. My son was killed three years ago on Cyterion-3." The colonel paused and turned away, his eyes unfocused. "I was informed two days ago of my daughter's death ... well, probable death. Her platoon was overrun. The battalion retook the position later, but there were no bodies to..."

The colonel's voice trailed off and they sat in silence, Tyko's eyes darting from the image of the young woman to the colonel's face. The senior officer turned and placed the image frame back on his desk, carefully adjusting the rectangular device so it would face him when he sat there again.

"You see, Flight Officer Tyko, the Vyps don't leave bodies behind, ours or theirs. That's not covered in your monthly training sessions, is it?" Tyko slowly shook his head as the colonel leaned forward. "Care to know why?"

Tyko felt light-headed and unsure of how to respond. The memory of his suspension being increased for asking questions about the war's beginning popped into his head. When he opened his mouth to reply his tongue felt two sizes too large. "Sir, I appreciate … uh, I'm not … uh … I don't believe that is information I am cleared to know."

"Once again, you speak the truth but without an answer." The colonel laughed bitterly. "Are you contemplating a career in politics, Tyko? Because if so, you've got a leg up on your peers."

The older man must have noticed the look of consternation on his face. "Sorry, son. No call for that. Your record is exemplary, even with that Pri-Fly business." The colonel leaned forward and placed a hand on Tyko's knee. He stared intently into the young pilot's eyes. "By the way, the same answer goes for both questions. Why do we keep pilots out of Pri-Fly and why we don't talk about the Vyps taking our dead and injured."

"Sir?" Tyko didn't know what to say, so he mumbled the first thing that came to mind.

"We don't want you to see what this war can, and likely will do to you." The colonel shook his head slowly from side to side. "We don't want you, or your families for that matter, to know because when almost all of you turn eighteen you'll leave this relatively safe base station and actually go to war. We don't want you to know because ideally we want you to *want to go* to the Expeditionary Forces. You'll learn different when you get there, but at that point … well, you're already there, aren't you?"

The colonel leaned back and massaged his forehead. "That's something else Fleet doesn't want you to know, Tyko. There isn't a tremendous need for pilots outside of these base stations. When I said almost all of you will go to Expeditionary, I mean about ninety-eight percent of you."

Tyko's mind whirled at this information. He had never paid much attention when pilots left his squadron, but had any of them transferred anywhere except to the ground forces? Had he heard of anyone from his Air Wing? No … and … no.

He cocked his head to the side and looked questioningly at the colonel. "Why are we told about all the different types of billets then, sir? Why bother?"

"To keep you from thinking about it. Oh, plenty of you put

in for one of those cushy jobs like instructor or staff officer, but somehow none of those postings are ever available when those people rotate. Well, almost never available. Transport pilots get killed often enough, but there are so many of you ..." The colonel stood and stretched, rolling his shoulders before turning back to face the pilot. "You're going to be seventeen in a few months, isn't that true?"

"Six months, sir." Tyko looked up at the older man, his complete confusion evident. "Colonel, is that why I'm here? Why you're telling me this?"

"Partially, yes."

"If what you say ... sorry, sir. Based on what you say, there is nothing I can do, so why tell me?" The colonel looked as if he was thinking about a response, and then Tyko remembered something else. "Besides, sir, the war may be over by then. I mean, we're not finding many Vyps to fight anymore."

The senior man shook his head. "Don't confuse their absence in this sector with an overall defeat." He looked down at the image frame. "There is no shortage of Vyps where my daughter was."

"Yes, sir." Tyko shifted in his seat, the softness of the cushions beginning to feel uncomfortable to a backside accustomed to hard composite everywhere from Fighter Control Units to mess hall benches. If the colonel was trying to test his loyalty, Tyko felt he had passed. If not ... well, the young pilot had no idea what the man was trying to tell him.

Either way, Tyko wanted to get back to the flight deck as soon as possible. "Colonel, you said that was partially the reason. Is there some other reason you wanted to talk to me?"

"Yes, there is." The older man nodded and crossed his arms. "Tell me about Flight Officer Caviness."

"Sir?" Tyko swallowed hard, a sinking feeling in the pit of his stomach. *Have I somehow gotten Caviness in trouble?*

After their first kiss, being with Caviness supplanted everything else in Tyko's mind. He studied her schedule, looking for windows of opportunity. He missed meals, went without sleep, to spend a few minutes with her. And then one entire, wonderful, day together when their watch rotations finally aligned: three meals, a walk around the station, time in the rec hall and capped off with a vid marathon.

They messaged each other at least once daily, with Tyko hearing her voice in his mind as he read the words.

"You two have become quite close, based on observation and your correspondence."

Tyko's face grew warm. *Why didn't I tell her our messages are monitored?* He had quit thinking about it, deciding instead to enjoy what was happening rather than worry about potential consequences. In doing so, had he condemned them both? His heart began to sink at the prospect.

The colonel picked up a datapad from the desk. He glanced at it for a moment. "For quite some time you've been evaluated as having interest only in yourself, which isn't uncommon in your age group. When you connected with her it was somewhat of a surprise to your squadron support cadre."

The colonel did not acknowledge his questioning look. "It is important and good for you to begin sharing more of yourself with others. Emotionally, and, in time, physically. Those connections are a big part of what makes us human."

Tyko's uneasiness faded a bit. "Before I met ... well, before I was focused on my flying. And the war. Sir."

"Yes, your record indicates that." The senior officer glanced down at the datapad. "Analysis of the messages between yourself and Officer Caviness indicates a, ah, certain ... maturity. Where many of your peers simply look for casual enjoyment, the two of you appear to have formed a deeper connection."

The colonel leaned back against the desk, his eyes fixed on Tyko's. "There are provisions in Fleet regs for flight officers to sign commitment contracts once they've turned seventeen. As you know, the single greatest advantage the Vyps have over us is their birthrate. They outnumber us on every battlefield." Tyko's eyes darted to the back of the image frame, suddenly thankful he couldn't see the face of the woman whose platoon had been overrun. "This provision recognizes the high priority we as humans must place on creating new life."

"I see." But even as he said it, Tyko thought of the others in his squadron his age or older. Did any of them seem remotely capable of being parents? Did he?

The colonel sensed his thoughts."There is a probation period in the commitment contract for those younger than the age of full consent. To be honest with you, from the statistics most of these contracts never make it past the probationary period, but ... well, as I said earlier: there appears to be something *more* between the two of you. I thought it worth discussing with you."

Tyko nodded and licked his lips. "Thank you, sir. I'll, um, think about what you've said."

"Good. She should also be having this same discussion with someone in her chain of command." The colonel placed the datapad on the desk and as his drew his hand back his fingers brushed the image frame. "The recommendation crossed my desk a couple days ago, and I decided to speak to you about it myself."

There was a moment of silent before the older officer's face visibly brightened.

"Just so you know, too, if the two of you sign a contract I've convinced the Air Group Commander to transfer you to a squadron in Third Wing on the same watch rotation. Between us, Third can use your help." He grinned conspiratorially. "We can't put the two of you in the same squadron, of course, but you wouldn't have to miss meals or leave your teammates shorthanded on the quantam court to spend a few minutes with her anymore."

For the third time in half an hour Tyko's head began to swim.

Seeing Caviness every day, spending nearly every off-patrol minute together, would have been his first wish if the Fleet granted such things to sixteen-year-old pilots. But signing a commitment contract had never occurred to him. Commitment was a big step ... a *huge* step. Old people were committed to each other, like his parents and the neighbors on either side of their house. His primary school headmaster and grandparents — they were committed. He and Caviness were too young to even think about it.

But ... what if she *had* thought of it? Were they close enough yet that she would tell him?

Commitment implied a lifelong bond, which he liked the idea of the more he thought about it, but also ... children. One of them could use a child to defer their military service, but would they? He didn't think so, which meant either her grandparents on Barribes or his parents on New Earth would raise the baby.

The baby. A baby. Our baby.

Tyko involuntarily shuddered. *Am I already thinking like this is happening?*

The colonel's voice brought him out of his reverie. "It's a lot to take in, I know. No decisions need be made, soon or ever actually. The option is there. Her birthday is only a few weeks after yours, so once you turn eighteen it would be easy enough to transfer you both to either New Earth or Barribes for the usual eight months."

The officer sat back and smiled. "Of course, if you two don't conceive naturally in that time, there are other options. Creating new children has the highest priority."

Caviness. Home. Commitment. Kids. The meeting with the colonel felt like a dream of some kind. Or maybe a nightmare.

When he spoke, he tried to keep his voice steady, but wasn't sure how successful he was. "Thank you, sir. I'll think about this, talk to Caviness, when, er, if ... well, at some point."

"Good. I'm glad we had this chance to talk." The colonel's gaze drifted to the back of the image frame on his desk. When he continued, his voice sounded remote. "If either of you have questions, take them to your squadron support officers."

Realizing he'd been dismissed, Tyko got up and quickly left the colonel's stateroom.

A Journey Ends

R his spent much of the first two days in the cell pacing from one end to the other. That wasn't very far, given the room was just a bit smaller than the one-man ship he was in when the Vyptellians captured him.

As cells went, this one was comfortable enough. At least Rhis imagined it to be so, as he had never been a part of the penal system on New Earth. The walls were a light blue color, the smooth floor a deep brown. The temperature was cool but not uncomfortably so, and the air was heavy with moisture as if he were near a large body of water. On one end of the rectangular space was a small settee and armchair; on the opposite side were a narrow cot and the curtained opening to a tiny water closet. In the center of the room was a small table with two chairs.

He sat at the table, facing the only door. In front of him were a cup and a tray with the remnants of his breakfast. At any moment he expected the door to open and his alien jailer to enter. *This time*, Rhis thought, *I must make it understand I'm not just another prisoner.*

But when the door finally opened it was an elderly human woman who walked into the cell. The surprise Rhis felt seeing the woman quickly turned to outright shock when he recognized her as Professor Sanfinagalo, one of his instructors at the Diplomatic University.

"Hello, Rhis. I am sorry you had to wait but I was off-planet," she said, pulling out the chair across from him and sitting down.

"But ... you're *dead*!"

The gray-haired professor smiled gently. "So I've been told."

* * * *

After launching from Talmeoud-2, the small ship carrying Rhis followed a pre-programmed flight path into Vyptellian-controlled space, broadcasting a message identifying its passenger as an emissary of New Earth. The broadcast was in three parts, with the same phrase transmitted in Earth Common, Hrustian and what Rhis fervently hoped was an accurate translation of Vyptellian.

Two weeks later a proximity alarm alerted Rhis to the presence of another vessel. The Vyptellians brought his ship inside one of their own and when two lights on the small control display flashed green, indicating a breathable atmosphere outside, he opened the main hatch as he had been taught.

With legs shaking so hard he could barely walk, he stepped out of the ship in front of more than a dozen heavily armed and armored Vyptellian soldiers. In one hand was a datapad with a translation application activated and in the other was a pad with an open file displaying Vyptellian characters that he had been told were a formal request to meet with the Vyptellian government.

Two Vyptellians grabbed him roughly by the arms and another took the pads from him before his feet touched the deck. His voice shaking and hoarse with fear, Rhis tried to communicate with them, telling them his name and that he was an emissary of New Earth, but they ignored his pleas. He was placed in a small compartment that appeared to be a medical facility and then left mostly alone for the trip to his present location. Rhis estimated the journey took four days, based on the number of times they tried to feed him a foul-smelling gray paste.

He had no idea if the cell was on a space station, planet, or moon. Three Vyptellians escorted him from the medical compartment to an exit hatch that opened on a large enclosed docking bay. There he was handed over to two other Vyps, who were unarmed. These aliens led him from the docking bay to the cell through nondescript corridors that were irregularly lined by doors and empty of other life.

* * * *

"I attended your remembrance at the university! We, we were told you died, in a fall, while hiking," Rhis sputtered, looking at the professor. "How is this possible?"

"Oh, but I do miss the wooded lands around New Melbourne." Sanfinagalo smiled wistfully before turning serious again. "Of course, I was never in those woods, and did not die there. That is just what was said to cover up my disappearance."

"What? Why?" Rhis felt his heart slow to near normal.

"Because you are the latest in a long line that began with me."

"You were an emissary?"

"The first, yes." The professor reached across the table and took one of his hands in both of hers. Her fingers were wrinkled and spotted with age. "I was found by the Vyptellians about fifteen years ago, much farther from here than where you were intercepted."

Rhis felt a dawning realization pass over him. "We heard … there were rumors … of a peace mission after the war started, but the Council … well, there were warnings to never speak of it."

Sanfinagalo shook her head and her tone sharpened. "I am not surprised. I imagine you were told you would be the first?" He nodded. "Yes, that is what they always say. The Council sends an emissary every few years. Most are still alive and you will meet them in due time."

"Most … are still alive?"

"Mmm. The Vyptellians had nothing to do with those who died, I can assure you. One took sick and another committed suicide." The old professor's tone softened. "They were the second and third emissaries after me, respectively. It has not been easy being so far from home, with no contact. I myself have no family, but Nguyen and Sestra … well, it was very hard for them. As the war continued more prisoners were taken and now we have quite a thriving community here for support, including some doctors. Still, for many it is very difficult."

Listening to her, Rhis suddenly felt his chest tighten and his vision narrow to pinpoints filled by the professor's face, which registered her sudden concern. He was only dimly aware of his hand slipping out of hers, or her calling out his name, as he fell from the chair.

* * * *

When he came to, Rhis was on the cot, a damp cloth across his brow. Professor Sanfinagalo sat next to him in one of the chairs pulled over from the table. Standing in the doorway was the Vyptellian he thought of as his jailer.

"How long?" His voice was small, like a child's.

"Just a few minutes," the professor replied, her face sympathetic. "I am sorry. Everyone deals with the situation differently. I should have gone slower."

"How did I ... did the Vyptellian move me?"

"I certainly didn't. My days of carrying men to bed are long past." She laughed and he smiled weakly. Her face grew serious. "You'd still be on the floor if he wasn't accustomed to dealing with us. This is an induction center. Most Vyptellians abhor physical contact with humans."

Rhis sat up, grabbing the damp cloth as it slipped from his forehead. "May I ask a question?"

"I imagine you have many!"

"If you made contact with the Vyptellians fifteen years ago, if all the emissaries made contact, why have there been no peace talks?" A sudden thought struck him and he started. "Or have there?"

"No, no talks." The old woman leaned back in her chair. "There have been no talks because the Vyptellians do not believe in negotiated settlements to end wars. There can only be victory or defeat. That is their custom."

"Oh." Rhis swung his legs out and placed his feet on the floor. He looked at the professor. "That must have been very difficult for you to accept. I recall your lectures on communication as a key factor in diplomacy."

"Yes, I spent years trying to convince the Vyptellians to open a dialog with New Earth. But ... can a mountaineer reason with an avalanche?" Sanfinagalo leaned forward in the chair, placing both hands on her knees. "This room is so small. Would you care to get some fresh air?"

He looked at the Vyptellian and then back at her. "May we?"

The professor laughed and held out a hand. "Come on, then. Let me show you a little of where you'll live out the war."

She said something in a language he guessed to be Vyptellian and the alien in the doorway stepped aside to let them pass. It followed them as the professor led him down a corridor and to a door. She pulled the door open, flooding the corridor with light, and they walked out onto an open plaza facing a large emerald-green lake lined by trees and low bushes. Rhis sighed with appreciation as a gentle, fragrant breeze caressed his face.

A dozen humans were in the plaza, standing or sitting alone or in groups. Many appeared to be recovering from injuries, with bandaged limbs or nearby medical stands. A few looked up at Rhis and the professor but most were too deeply involved in their thoughts or conversations. Sanfinagalo pointed to an empty bench made from a composite material and they sat; Rhis noticed his jailer remained inside the building, and no other Vyptellians were visible.

The professor gestured at the plaza with an open hand. "This particular compound is for high ranking civilian and military personnel. We are just a short distance from the center of their capital city. There are other, much larger, settlements for general prisoners on planets throughout the Vyptellia system."

"You said you were off-planet, is that where you were?"

"Oh yes, I make the rounds regularly. I suppose you could say the Vyptellians recognize me as humanity's representative." She suddenly laughed. "Unelected, of course. The military would never stand for it otherwise. But, the Vyptellians did the choosing, not them."

The professor gazed out at the lake. "Whatever they told you about the Vyptellians, I have no doubt it was not everything we've learned about the species. The Council and Military Command keep a lot of what they know to themselves."

"I believe that."

Sanfinagalo sighed. "Governments keeping secrets is a legacy of Old Earth, one that we thought was behind us before the Long Exodus." She turned to look him in the eyes. "We also believed we were done starting wars. How foolish we were to forget our past."

"Did they? Are you sure? Some of us who were alive then may remember what we've been encouraged to forget, but is it the whole truth? It certainly is not the truth the Vyptellians know."

Rhis sighed and his shoulders slumped. "Does it even matter at this point?"

The professor glanced sideways at him. "I believe it does. There is an Old Earth saying: those who do not learn from the past are fated to repeat it."

"Mmmm."

She placed a gnarled hand on his shoulder and smiled sadly. "Practically speaking, you are correct. It does not matter. Remembering how a war started is the prerogative of the winning side. Soon this war will be over and humanity will become subject to Vyptellian rule, joining many other species, including the Hrustians."

"The Hrustians?" His jaw dropped.

"Yes, the Vyptellians conquered Hrus several hundred years ago." Her tone shifted to that of the university lecturer he remembered. "Vyptellian culture is based on martial prowess to a large degree, but they are not harsh overlords. Once an enemy is defeated or captured, they are treated with honor and respect, and it is Vyptellian practice to return subjects to self-rule as soon as possible. In time, as long as the subject planet or planets pay tribute, the Vyptellians leave them be."

His brow wrinkled. "The Hrustians are pacifists, they don't even have a military. How could they possibly fight a war with the Vyptellians?"

"Obviously since they lost, they didn't pose much of a challenge!" Sanfinagalo laughed quietly. "This was centuries ago. Our ancestors were still killing each other on Old Earth. Much can change, can it not, in that time? As for a military, Hrus does not need one because it is protected by Vyptellia."

"Why would they not tell us if that was true?"

"Perhaps they did." The professor shrugged. "Perhaps we never asked. Would the Council have announced it either way? Honestly, I've always wondered about our relationship with Hrus. Did they truly give us faster-than-light travel of their own accord or did we extort it from them? Certainly the temptation was there. They had this wonderful technology. We had weapons, ostensibly for self-defense, and they were unarmed."

Rhis felt his head beginning to swim again. "S-sorry," he muttered, placing a hand on the bench to steady himself.

"No, that is quite all right," Sanfinagalo said with concern in her voice. "I'm prattling on and on, giving you a lot to take in all at once. And after such a long journey. I'm the one who should be sorry. I do hope you will forgive me."

They sat in silence for several minutes. At length, Rhis opened his eyes and looked at the lake. He noticed small dark specks circling above the green water and wondered if they were a type of bird.

"Are you feeling better now?"

"Yes, thank you."

"Good." Sanfinagalo nodded.

"You said the war would end soon. Why? How?"

Sanfinagalo stood and stretched. "When the incident at Nex Altrien happened the Vyptellians were already involved in a war on the other side of the galaxy."

Rhis blinked. "What?"

"Yes, they were fighting a species we have never met or even heard of." She motioned for him to get up and together they walked across the plaza. "The Vyptellians told me they did not want a conflict with us, at least not then, but their code of honor required a response."

At the end of the plaza was an unpaved path leading to the lake. The path wasn't wide enough for them to walk side by side so she took the lead, turning her head back as she continued speaking.

"The Vyptellians had more than a billion soldiers fighting this other war, but there were still more than enough to hold us back." They reached the end of the path and stood at the water's edge. Sanfinagalo turned to face him. "Vyptellians are quite clever. They took weapons and other items captured from our soldiers and copied them."

She faced the lake. "These weapons helped them to finally win their other war, several months ago. Now all those soldiers are moving against New Earth."

"Is there nothing we can do to stop it? To warn them?"

"I'm afraid not. But, hopefully it will be over soon and the killing can stop."

"What will happen to us?"

"I expect we prisoners will be returned to New Earth."

Rhis stood silently for several minutes, breathing in the tangy air and feeling the breeze off the water on his arms and face. Something the professor said earlier popped into his head, and he asked her about it.

* * * *

That evening Professor Sanfinagalo stopped by his room, enquiring if he wanted to have dinner with the other prisoners. Rhis thanked her but declined. His mood had been down since their talk at the lake and he didn't feel up to facing the barrage of questions the others would have.

The professor studied him for a moment, concern etched on her wrinkled brow. "I suppose one more night on your own won't matter too much."

"Thank you."

She turned to go but stopped suddenly. "Ah, I nearly forgot.

The name you asked me to check on."

"Yes?"

"There is no record of a prisoner by that name. I'm sorry."

"Oh." He slowly nodded. "I thought ... hoped ... well, if there was a chance."

She opened her mouth to reply but he began to shut the door.

"Thank you. Good night, professor."

An hour later Rhis stepped out into the corridor. Part of him expected the Vyptellian to be there to stop him, but the corridor was empty. Walking to the exit, he concluded the alien had likely only been there to watch him until the professor returned.

He left the building and crossed the plaza, following the path to the lake. The night air was cool against his skin but the breeze was gone. Two moons, one much brighter than the other, provided ample light to see by.

Rhis stood looking at the water for several minutes, listening to the soft slap of waves against the shore. He thought of the thousands killed in battle, the parents left childless and the children orphaned. He wondered what became of the child he selfishly refused to adopt, and what would happen to her under Vyptellian rule.

Hot tears began to roll down his cheeks.

His mind turned to Djovic, who died believing the war was just. Rhis had wanted to honor his partner's sacrifice, to atone for the shallowness of his own life by ensuring Djovic's death had meaning through the small part he would play in ending the war. But he failed. There would be no redemption, no great meaning to explain the loss of thousands of lives including the only person he ever loved.

The futility of it was overwhelming.

Closing his eyes, Rhis walked into the lake, ignoring its icy chill as his head slid beneath the surface.

WHITE OSCAR FOUR ZERO

"White Oscar Four Zero, are you there?"

Tyko started, suddenly aware he'd been deep in his own thoughts and had missed flight control's call.

"Control, uh, White Oscar Four Zero. Sorry. Still getting used to the new call sign."

"White Oscar Four Zero, understood." One of the positives of moving to Third Wing, Tyko thought with a small smile, was flight control officers who were less concerned with military protocol. "You're hard against the flick, Four Zero. Bring them back toward the station and continue patrol. Time to bingo one hour."

"Roger, control. My scans are clear across the board."

"Four Zero, our scans are clear as well."

The Forward Line of Communication Connectivity, know as the flick, was the theoretical limit for remotely piloted fighters. After reporting to the station Tyko heard flight deck rumors that the flick was determined less by technical requirements than the Air Group's whims, but whichever was true no pilot wanted to lose a fighter finding out.

Tyko ordered the other seven fighters with him to execute a long, gentle turn back toward the station. The patrol was as uneventful as the one the day before, and the day before that. In fact, more than two weeks had passed since Tyko or anyone in his squadron had encountered any Vyptellians, and that fight was over very quickly — four Vyps were no match for several squadrons of frustrated teenagers.

The base station had moved twice already and if Henrik was to be believed another move into Vyptellian territory was in the planning stages. Several days earlier Tyko and Caviness ran into Henrik and several of his former squadron mates in the passageway outside the station library. After exchanging greetings (and enduring the giggles of the younger pilots at the sight of the couple holding hands), Henrik leaned in and quietly told them about a meeting he attended in Fourth Wing's operations center. Walking back to the conference room, the young pilot studied the navigation and tactical plots on large datascreens at the front of the compartment.

"There was a row of base stations displayed, about ten, and we're third from the end on the starboard side," Henrik whispered, his eyes scanning the crowd passing by. Spreading rumors about tactical matters was something support officers would be on the lookout for. "A solid yellow line was drawn over the stations, and there were two dashed lines behind that and a blue line farther ahead. I think the dash lines are where we've been and the blue line is where we're going next. And it's *deep* inside Vyp territory. Well, what used to be theirs." He said this last bit with a smug smile.

Whether the support officers liked it or not, whether the Group or even Fleet liked it or not, there was no stopping the young pilots at the station from talking about the lack of enemy activity. At first there was concern that the Vyps were drawing them into a trap, but the days with few or no sightings stretched into a week, then two weeks. When they also considered the alien's recent change to remote piloting, many came to different conclusion: the Vyptellians were retreating.

A few mess hall admirals even began to make predictions about how much longer the war would last.

Tyko wasn't sure about any of that, but given all the recent changes in his life he wasn't unhappy with the lack of activity on patrol. He would prefer to be dueling Vyp fighters, sure, but lately he was reminded on a daily basis how much fun it was to just strap into the pilot's seat in a Fighter Control Unit, take command of a distant ship, and fly it around space.

After transferring to Third Wing, he spent nearly every waking minute outside of a control unit with Caviness. Tyko found this to be good and … slightly less than good. He wouldn't say it was bad, but it definitely was a change. A big change they agreed to make together, but he now knew her well enough to know she also felt the weight of how their relationship was evolving.

Relationship. Is that what we should call it? I'm still not sure, he thought, leading the patrol through a climbing turn.

A week after his meeting with the Air Group Support Officer, Tyko wasn't sure what to say to her about it. Their flight schedules were not in sync so they were communicating solely through nightly e-notes, which he knew were monitored. He typed out and deleted numerous notes during that time, never quite finding a way to put into words the colonel's suggestion that they consider a commitment contract.

Then one afternoon he entered his stateroom after coming off patrol to find the green light blinking on the network terminal, indicating her daily e-note was waiting in the queue. Expecting to spend a pleasant few moments with the closest approximation of her possible before grabbing some rack time, he was taken aback by what he read.

Typed in all-caps and heavily punctuated with question marks and exclamation points, Caviness wrote she had met that day with her squadron commander to discuss her future plans with Tyko. She made it clear she hadn't given any prior thought to the idea of committing to Tyko, or anyone else, and it was unlikely she would consider it at any point in the foreseeable future. She added some mildly disapproving words about her commander, whose idea she assumed the whole thing to be.

Tyko quickly typed a reply, telling her it was important they meet the next day. He would skip breakfast and be waiting when she got off patrol. Mindful of the other eyes reading their notes, he added a line that her commander was probably only doing what he thought best. He flagged the note URGENT and hit send, then spent a sleepless night tossing and turning in his bunk.

He didn't need it but there was a reminder that everything they did was watched the next morning: a support officer was waiting outside his berthing compartment.

"You're off the flight roster today, Tyko," she said, falling into step with him. "Take all the time you need."

Evidently, the colonel was more interested in seeing this happen than he originally thought. That idea worried him, but not as much as the thought of Caviness never wanting to see him again after he told her about his meeting with the colonel. There was much he didn't understand about his feelings toward her, but he knew he didn't want that.

By the time she came through the Third Wing flight deck hatch he was pacing, his stomach a knot of uncertainty. She smiled crookedly at him, one eyebrow pulled down with curiosity. Mindful of the stream of pilots and support officers moving back and forth through the double hatchway, she walked over and chastely touched his arm. Tyko never wanted to hold her more than he did just then.

"You have no idea how hard it was going through another

no-contact patrol after your reply last night. Soooo … what's so important?"

"Let's have breakfast. I know how hungry you are after patrol."

She took a short step back, dropping her hand from his arm. "What? Aren't you on duty in half an hour? We'll never get through the line."

"Don't worry, I'm off the roster." He nearly laughed as her jaw dropped. "C'mon, let's get some food. We can, uh, talk at the table. Okay?"

He led her into the mess hall. As they got into line and grabbed trays, Tyko focused on the comforting routine of the mess hall — shuffling slowly forward enveloped by the smells of cooked and cooking food, feeling the heat radiating from the galley, and hearing the low murmuring of hundreds of people. Some of his nervousness faded.

The respite was brief, though.

They found a small table in one corner and sat, their food instantly forgotten as they focused on each other. Caviness leaned in and slipped her hand into his, an encouraging half-smile on her face. Tyko's brain searched for the right way to begin and finally he just started talking, his thoughts out of order and making little sense to her. She stopped him, squeezed his hand, and told him to start over from the beginning.

He tried again, telling her about being called to meet with the Air Group colonel and what the officer said about the early commitment program. How as pilots they were monitored more by the support officers than she realized. That their private notes had been read and their meetings monitored, with everything put down into reports sent up to their Wings and the Air Group. He also told her about the way future postings were weighted toward the Expeditionary Corps, with almost no pilots continuing to fly after turning eighteen.

Caviness listened and said nothing, her face an emotionless mask. But she didn't take her hand from his, and he was glad for that.

When he asked her what she was thinking, Caviness shook her head. "Why would this man, a senior officer — who doesn't even know either of us — do this? That part I don't understand. That's *one* of the parts I don't understand."

Tyko said he wasn't sure, but thought it had something to do with the colonel's daughter being killed in action. "He got the

notice just before I was ordered to meet him. I don't know …
maybe he started thinking about his kids — his son was killed in
action, too — and we're supposed to replace them somehow."

"I don't want to have … I've never even thought about
children. Or commitment." His face must have fallen, because
she squeezed his hand. "It isn't you, Tyko. I like spending time
with you. But we're *sixteen*. All we've ever known is our
families, the Academy and this station. You're the best part of
right now, but … I don't know. I want to keep flying forever,
and I thought I would. I'd turn eighteen and be posted
somewhere, a planet or a different system and I'd actually *fly*,
you know?"

"I know what you're saying." He nodded. Paused. Decided
to not hold back. "But you should know in my perfect future I'm
also in that different system … and you're my co-pilot."

She snorted. "Your co-pilot? Try the other way around."

He laughed and she joined in, breaking the tension. She
squeezed his hand again. "So, what do we do about this? You
haven't said what you think of the idea. Don't just agree with
me, I'll know if you do."

"I like the idea of spending more time with you. Of not
having to wait a week to see you for a few minutes."

"I'd like that, too. You have to know I would."

"I do. Look, he said there's a way to get out of it. An opt-
out. Nothing is final." He shrugged. "You don't have to be stuck
with me, in other words."

Caviness picked up a fork and dragged it through the
congealing mush on her tray. After a few moments she looked
up with a grin. "I had an instructor at the Academy who told us
good deals are few and far between in the Fleet. When you get
one, grab it."

"I heard that, too. Probably from the same guy."

"If there really is a way out, maybe we tell them yes and
then see what happens. With us, I mean."

"Yeah?"

"Yeah. No promises, though. Okay?"

"Sure. No promises."

The fork stopped moving as she suddenly grew serious.
"Hey! You'll change squadrons. And Wings. Are you going to
be okay with that?"

"I will." Tyko nodded to reassure her. He reached out for the
glass on his tray. Lifting it to his mouth he casually added, "I'd

rather kiss you than Henrik."

She laughed so loud pilots at nearby tables stopped eating to look over at them.

That had been two weeks ago. He made the move to Third Wing four days later and quickly realized how much he had taken for granted being in the same squadron, same wing, for more than three years.

In theory Fleet procedures were the same everywhere but in reality there were subtle differences, and it was made clear that any adjustments were his to make. He was told to forget the ways things were done 'downstairs' and warned against suggesting any changes to conform to how his previous unit operated.

He also had to learn the strengths and weaknesses of his new squadron mates so he'd know who he could rely on in a fight.

Of course there were the questions from pilots and support officers about the reason for his transfer and his connection with Caviness. Even his new squadron commander gave the impression she thought Tyko's transfer was more due to the Wing's concerns about her leadership abilities than an obscure Fleet regulation.

Their schedules didn't exactly line up as the colonel had suggested, but he was still getting to spend a lot of time with Caviness and both were happy about that. Other than being with her, next best for him was climbing into a control unit for patrol duty. That there were no Vyps to fight mattered less to him than a temporary escape from stumbling around like a fresh-from-the-Academy newcomer.

"White Oscar Four Zero this is Control. You are bingo plus ten minutes but relieving squadron is on station at this time. You can bring them home a little early."

"This is Four Zero. If it's all the same we'll finish what we started."

"Roger that, Four Zero."

Tyko grinned behind his faceshield. The other pilots on patrol with him were no doubt grumbling but he didn't care. Ten minutes? He'd fly the next patrol cycle if they let him.

Shipping Over

Lieutenant Bokamu saw the flashing icon as soon as he pulled the datapad from its place on his belt.

He already knew it would be there. Two weeks earlier the icon first appeared in green, a visual cue telling him there was an action item from the Group in his admin queue. A few days later the icon turned to yellow, as if to say: *Not sure how, but maybe you didn't see this yet, eh Lieutenant?*

A few more days passed and the color changed again, to red, and the icon began flashing.

Floating behind the on-watch team, securely strapped in and intently focused on their readouts, datascreens, and displays, he stared at the red flash and inwardly sighed. Grabbing a handhold he twisted around and pulled himself forward, easily floating toward the opposite end of the pod that was one of New Earth's most secret military projects and his home for the past eighty-three days, nine hours and thirty-three minutes.

Bokamu was technically the officer in charge of the pod, designated *Heimdallr Eight*, but his position seemed more like that of a school teacher or — worse — parent. He far out-ranked the pod's six other occupants, two men and four women, but it was their skill and knowledge that was crucial to the mission, not his. They had been hand-picked for the task, plucked from what he assumed were the deep ranks of Military Command's intelligence community.

He was told his selection was just as carefully made, but Bokamu quickly realized it wasn't for his martial qualities. One of the few to remain on flight status after attaining the age of majority, Bokamu was an instructor at the Academy when the two colonels from the Active Intelligence Group came to see him. Yes, he was a good pilot and they played up the need for those skills in their new project. But, more important to them (he later learned) was his demonstrated ability to lead and guide cadets, who as newly-turned adolescents were frequently truculent, moody, and unfocused.

Truculent and moody certainly characterized the team of specialists with him on *Heimdallr Eight*, but if anything they were too focused. This was especially true of Pemberton, the reason for the flashing icon and the man Bokamu headed aft to find.

Of the six specialists, Pemberton was undoubtedly the best. He was the most proficient in the basics of Vyptellian language and could also draw inferences and conclusions from the communication intercepts, often with a startling degree of specificity. The slight, undernourished-looking man examined not only what the Vyps were saying and how, but also what was not being said.

Bokamu found him in the training room, deeply in thought while methodically placing one magnetic-booted foot in front of the other on the treadmill. He cleared his throat to get Pemberton's attention.

Pemberton glanced at him and said, "I miss having a choice."

Bokamu nodded. "We all do. But there's no getting around this. Just put your thumb on the screen and we can talk about anything else you want to."

"I just don't understand why it's necessary."

The lieutenant took a deep, calming breath. They'd had this same conversation so many times already. "You know I don't either. It just is. Next time the Supreme Commander or the Deputy or one of the Vice Commanders asks, I'll let them know we think it should be changed."

"You do that and they're likely to send you off to some far-off, isolated post." Pemberton smirked. "But that's the point, isn't it? Once you're inducted, they do whatever they want. Having us voluntarily re-enlist every few years, that's just part of the plan to make sure we know who's running our lives. As if we didn't already."

Secretly, Bokamu thought there might be something to what Pemberton was saying. Volunteer or drafted, once in the military there was a clause in the paperwork that said you were in for the duration of the war and whatever additional time Command felt necessary after hostilities ended. Even with that, every four years each of them was required to bio-metrically sign a document formally extending their service another four years.

The lieutenant tamped down his rising anger. The close quarters of the pod and somewhat boring routine (after the initial surge of adrenaline wore off) combined with Pemberton's natural smugness was a recipe for a confrontation that he, as the officer in charge, needed to avoid. He took another deep breath before continuing.

"Look, all I'm saying ... all I've *been* saying, is even if you don't sign it nothing changes. You're not going anywhere. You know this, Pemberton."

"I know it."

"So ... sign already. Do it for me. I need it off my action list."

The slight man stared at the bulkhead for a few moments, his legs and arms silently moving back and forth. He turned back to the lieutenant with a crooked smile. "I've got a few more days until it *has* to be signed, right?" Without wanting to, Bokamu nodded. "I'll do it on the day then. No sense in giving them anything extra, am I right?"

"You wouldn't be giving anyone anything extra doing it now."

"No, but doing it when I decide makes me feel like I have a little control over my life again. What's the harm in that?"

"Well, I could report you for conduct detrimental to the war effort. The penalty for that would eat up your next two enlistments."

Pemberton's smile disappeared and he stopped in place, one arm swung out in front, the other back. "Aw, you're a good officer, lieutenant. You've been good to us out here and all. You wouldn't do that."

"It may not matter. Some bright mind at Group will notice how long this sat on my action list." Bokamu lifted an eyebrow. "Then they'll ask me about it and you know I'm not going to admit it was my fault it didn't get done right away."

The specialist's arms and legs began to slowly move again as the ends of his lips curved upwards. "No, I suppose you wouldn't, would you? Well, in that case the cards are dealt and I'm already in trouble, right? So, I'm going to just play it out and hope for the best. There's a good chance none of us are getting back, anyway. Given where we are and all."

Heimdallr Eight was positioned just inside a large system with four planets inhabited by Vyptellians, hiding in a small field of asteroids. The pod and its tow ship traveled deep into Vyp-controlled space, approaching its destination from what the Group colonels confidently called 'the back door' — a sector that had seen little activity from either side. At a designated point the pod was released and it continued gliding forward for another ten days until Bokamu used maneuvering jets to slow and then stop it among the asteroids.

The Group colonels said the system where *Heimdallr Eight* was stationed, designated Victor Charlie-3, was one of the alien race's core locations in the galaxy — perhaps even the Vyptellian home system (*how* they knew this — well, he knew better than to ask). They told Bokamu the Heimdallr project was of vital importance to the survival of humanity, and that he believed. He wasn't sure how many listening stations there were (he assumed at least eight, but who knew with intel types?) or how many were inside Victor Charlie-3, but he knew putting a surveillance post on the enemy's doorstep was worth the danger involved.

And *Heimdallr Eight* was a very sophisticated surveillance post, passively intercepting all manner of Vyptellian communications from the moment they activated the collection sensors attached to the pod's hull. Some intercepts were encrypted and obviously military in origin, but much of what they collected was not; after just a few days, Pemberton — who Bokamu learned was not one for hyperbole — opined the collected data amounted to a tripling of humanity's knowledge of Vyptellian society.

The movement of Vyp ships throughout the system was also captured and cataloged by optical sensors, with the vid feeds viewed on the main display on the command deck. Bokamu was told privately having such a 'window' on the outside would be important to the pod crew's mental stability, but it also provided the tensest moments of his life when a large Vyptellian ship came to a stop just a few thousand kilometers from their position. He shut down most systems and ordered everyone into their self-contained environmental suits (which was more for their mental state than a practical alternative). For several hours the seven of them floated in a group watching the display until the Vyp vessel suddenly began to move away from them.

Command wasn't exactly sure what sensor capabilities the Vyps possessed, so the pod was designed to look on visual, passive, and active scans like one of the asteroids it was hiding amidst. Solar panels captured enough energy from the system's star to provide for the sensor equipment and some housekeeping, but there was no artificial gravity and the temperature inside the pod was quite cold. Crew amenities were limited to lights, a small galley to warm food packets and drinks, the workout area, and heated bunks. Most of the pod was storage and equipment.

Pemberton and the other specialists stood eight-hour watches in pairs while Bokamu monitored them. Once a day, he downloaded the collected data onto a probe half the size of his datapad. After the probe was launched it was programmed to change course several times over a two-day period to foil any attempt to locate its point of origin (assuming the Vyps detected the launch) before transmitting the data on an encrypted frequency.

Bokamu studied the face of the man on the treadmill. He realized Pemberton was changing the subject and decided to indulge him for the moment. "You're still convinced something's going on with the Vyps?"

"Yes. As I've told you, it isn't the quantity of their broadcasts, that's only changed a bit in two-plus months. It's the *what*, not the *how much* they're saying, if you get me."

The lieutenant sighed. "We're capturing more data now than when we got here."

"True. But less of the encrypted stuff and more and more of the same civvie junk. Product ads, comms between family members ..."

"I suppose that could indicate they suspect we're listening."

"Yes."

"Maybe their communications run in cycles. Ours do. Maybe it's a Vyp holiday, or the schools are on hiatus."

"Sure. Or maybe they're planning something and don't want us to know." Pemberton passed his hand over the treadmill's control pad, stopping the machine. "Visual is also capturing a lot more ship traffic between the planets and through the system, and fighter patrols."

"I've noticed that."

"Did you notice they haven't come out this way again? Not since that one time."

"Well, this position was carefully chosen." Pemberton smirked and Bokamu fought back the urge to snap something back about respecting the competency of senior officers. "If they thought we were out here and wanted to feed us disinformation don't you think the amount of encrypted data would go up, not down?"

Pemberton's smirk faded and he bent over to unstrap the

mag boots. "Maybe. Yes. No. Maybe," he mumbled. Straightening up, he pushed off the bulkhead and floated in Bokamu's direction. "The fact is we still don't know very much about them. How they think, what they're likely to do."

He grabbed a bar to stop himself short of bumping into the lieutenant. Pemberton's crooked smile returned. "And by 'we' I mean us, out here. I'm sure somewhere in the bureaucracy there's a lab, with some captured Vyps and scientists who—"

Bokamu opened his mouth to cut Pemberton off but suddenly the lights in the training room switched to red and two low chimes sounded. The lieutenant grabbed a handrail and twisted his body around to face the command deck as Pemberton pulled himself past. In seconds both arrived at the same point behind the watch team.

"What do you have?" Bokamu scanned the main display.

The watch supervisor, a woman a few years older than him, pointed. "Three ships from the leftmost planet, heading directly towards us. CBDR."

Before the lieutenant could reply, the other watchstander muttered, "What the —" Her hands began to move across the controls of the console as she stared at the data readouts. Her eyes went wide. "I can't ... I don't *believe* this!"

"What is it?"

"Ships. Hundreds ... no, *thousands* of ships. Long range visual sensors have them ... they're ... they're —" The specialist gulped and her eyes darted to the main display. "They're coming from all four planets, and ... and from outside the system... more and more of them. It's not stopping!"

Bokamu looked up but didn't see anything other than three bright dots in the middle of the screen. Then the tech cycled the vid feed to long range and he saw a shining mass stretching like a ribbon through the system.

The lieutenant turned to the watch supervisor. "How soon until the initial three contacts arrive?" He was surprised at how calm he sounded; his stomach felt hollow. *There is no way out of this.*

"Approximately ten minutes. Sir?" The look on her face was grim. "What do we do? What can we do?"

He thought for a moment, remembered the worst-case scenarios they trained for. Out of the corner of his eye he saw the other three off-watch specialists gathered at the command deck entrance. "Let's get everyone into full enviro suits. We'll power down, play dead. We're close to the natural exit point for this end of the system. Maybe these three are the vanguard and they'll just go past."

Pemberton put a hand on Bokamu's arm. "We should warn them. Command. Tell them about this huge fleet."

The watch supervisor looked up, her eyes flashing. "If we launch a probe they'll know exactly where we are."

The specialist next to her switched the main display back to standard mode. The three bright spots had grown appreciably larger. "They already know where we are," she flatly stated.

"The Vyps travel faster than a probe," the watch supervisor continued, her tone sharp. "The data won't be sent for two days, it won't get there in time. Or they'll just blast the probe to dust."

"We can set the probe to begin transmitting as soon as it launches." Pemberton leaned over and began cycling through menus on the console, occasionally using one hand to keep himself from floating away. "I'm prepping the file for download, lieutenant. Get the launch menu up on your pad."

Bokamu stared at the three people clustered around the console, studying their faces: the watch supervisor and specialist looked very scared while Pemberton seemed totally calm. "Immediate broadcast means the Vyps will absolutely know where we are. You know that, right? There's a chance they don't —"

Pemberton shook his head. "They know we're here. I bet my life on it."

"You're betting all our lives," the watch supervisor hissed.

"Its like I was telling the lieutenant before. The cards are dealt. Let's make the best play we can." Pemberton shrugged. "Ready to launch."

A whirl of thoughts went through Bokamu's mind.

I'll never be committed to anyone.

I'll never have children.

I'll never see New Earth or my family again.

He looked at Pemberton — smirking, insolent, crooked-smiling Pemberton — and saw complete certainty in the man's face. Bokamu exhaled, and felt some of the fear rumbling through his body evaporate.

He raised the datapad and noticed the flashing red icon. A bitter laugh bubbled up his throat as he held a fingertip on the icon then swiped across 'cancel/ uncompleted' when the menu bubble appeared. Having put his admin house in order, Bokamu accessed the probe control function menu, finding a flashing green icon marked 'launch.'

Fifteen minutes later *Heimdallr Eight* was boarded by the Vyptellians.

MAKING IT COUNT

"I'm going to die," the second lieutenant said, his voice toneless. "What a stupid way to have to die."

Sergeant Siengha looked up but the officer's words weren't directed at her. Instead, he stared into the distance, the exhaustion every surviving member of the platoon felt making his face as devoid of emotion as his voice. She took one more glance at the young officer's armor control chipset, located on his right hip, and slowly shook her head.

Small, no bigger around than Siengha's little finger and just three millimeters thick, the chipset was nestled under one corner of an armor plate and accessible only through a hardened lid. It controlled several key features of a soldier's armor, including masking the human body's heat signature. Soldiers were told Vyptellian hunter drones searched for and locked in on human-sized hot or cold spots, depending on the surrounding environment

As much as she may have wanted to, there was no way to dispute the lieutenant's assessment. Tiny as it was, the lieutenant's chipset had shattered into three pieces after a direct hit on the armored lid. She shook her head again. In all the battles she had been part of, Siengha had never seen a control chipset destroyed before: it was a million-to-one shot.

The sergeant stood and stretched, her eyes checking the time displayed on the inside of her faceshield before sweeping the tight perimeter. They were in a narrow valley, just a slit between two stony hills. What was left of the platoon after the Towers battle — about twenty soldiers in all — sat with backs against dull red rock, chests heaving and limbs limp after two days of running from Vyp drones and cannon fire. They'd rested five minutes and she had planned on giving them five more; ahead was another day on the move to reach the latest rally point broadcast over the command net.

As much as she wanted to, Siengha hadn't dropped to the ground or leaned against the rocks when they reached this spot. Instead, she sipped water from the tube in her helmet while going from soldier to soldier, checking their status. Most had blunt impact wounds, their armor dented and scratched, and a few nursed broken bones, but nothing that impacted their mobility.

Then she got to the lieutenant, who at first tried to shoo her away and then ordered her to leave him alone. Siengha would have none of it.

"How long?" The officer didn't reply so she reached out and gave his shoulder a shake. He started and looked up at her. "How long have you known about the chip?"

"Does it matter?"

Siengha sighed. She liked this lieutenant as much as any the green officers Command sent to learn from her. He had been a flight officer and was selected for officer school after completing basic training, arriving at Operating Post Tango-5 with a large group of replacement soldiers just before the Vyp pull back. She spent the next ten days teaching him as much as she could about leading troops in battle, all the while growing more and more concerned about what the enemy was up to.

Unlike too many before him, this young officer listened attentively to everything she said, asked good questions, and checked with her before making decisions. When it was announced that a large force, including their platoon, was going to sortie from the outpost in search of the enemy, Siengha felt she and the lieutenant had formed a functional partnership that gave all of them a reasonable chance of survival in a fight.

But no matter how much she taught them the true test of any new soldier was battle, and at the Towers the lieutenant performed well. When the Vyps suddenly attacked, pouring through gaps in the rocky hills and from hidden pits, there was a brief moment when the young officer's fear got the best of him, but then it was over and he set about helping her get the platoon positioned and returning fire.

Penned into a valley by the two largest mountains in the region — the Towers — the human force quickly dug in and used pre-registered cannon fire and massed missile salvos from drones to hold off the initial assault waves. The aliens withdrew and used their own cannons and drones to batter the makeshift perimeter before launching another assault that nearly broke the human line in several places.

Siengha's platoon held firm but the unit to their right began to falter and she quickly formed a quick reaction team of five veteran soldiers to help them out. One of the five was shot down while shifting positions but the others jumped into the fray, which in places had become a hand-to-hand battle. At one point Siengha speared the midsection of Vyp with her assault rifle, fired several rounds, and then pushed the alien's lifeless body back to block two more who were then cut down by fire from the human line.

Shooting, using their rifles as clubs, and finally pulling out the combat blades sheathed on their lower legs, the sergeant and her team pushed back the attackers and sealed the breach — temporarily. The aliens fell back, pounded the humans with more cannon and drone fire, and then pushed forward again. And again.

Despite all the missiles and cannon shells fired into the massed aliens, their numbers never seemed to decrease. After an hour of battle the humans were exhausted and nearly out of ammunition; air assets, transports and assault ships, were called in to effect a breakout. The aliens had anticipated this and were prepared. As the last burning transport fell from the sky the ground commander came on the net and told company and platoon leaders to stand by to move.

Then the surviving assault ships used flamebombs to carve escape channels through the massed Vyps. One of the channels was directly in front of Siengha's position and as the assault ships screamed overhead she and the lieutenant led their platoon between the sheets of flame, shooting down any Vyps in their path. Others followed in their wake, but her focus was on what lay ahead.

She kept the group moving after escaping the killing field, allowing them only brief stops for rest. They heard drones overhead and cannonades fell all around them, some far away and some frighteningly close. As they moved, so too did the rally point, always to positions farther away from the battle.

Now with another day of running ahead of them, Siengha's face was devoid of emotion as she looked down at the young officer whose eyes were wet with unshed tears.

"It matters," she said in a quiet but firm voice.

The lieutenant's back straightened and he nodded. "Yeah, you're right. The last cannonade, where the trails crossed. I felt something hit my legs, but nothing made it through. There was a fault warning up on my display, but we were moving fast, making time. I figured it could wait 'til we stopped." He sighed. "I'm sorry. I should've said something right away."

Siengha nodded. She had to assume the Vyps were tracking them and had been for at least two hours, unseen drones zeroing in on the officer's heat signature. That they hadn't been shelled again meant either the aliens were hoping they would join more survivors of the Towers ambush to make a more enticing target for cannon fire, or ground troops were closing in.

Whichever it was, the sergeant knew what had to happen next. She switched to the platoon net. "Break's over. Everybody up and moving."

Ignoring the grumbling, she returned to the command channel and stepped in front of the lieutenant, placing herself between him and the others. "Okay, sir, this is what's going to happen. You stay here for another five to ten minutes after we leave, then head down our trail. There's a crossing on the nav display about a klick from here; you take the left trail, and then the next left after that."

"What? Look, maybe the chip doesn't do anything at all to spoof their drones. Maybe Command lied to us about it, you know, to make us feel safer." His eyes were desperate, pleading. "How would we know any different?"

She looked away from him, unable in that moment to watch him grovel.

There was a part of her that distrusted the tech, too. That didn't believe humanity's better gadgets would be the difference in winning the war. From what she'd seen, the only sure way to victory was through things that demonstrably killed and wounded the enemy, like bullets, knives, cannons and missiles.

But the battlefield was no place for philosophical discussions.

Siengha locked eyes with the lieutenant. "You're going to stay here for five or ten minutes, then follow on our path." Her tone was firm, unwavering. "Take the left trail about a klick along, then the next left."

The lieutenant's shoulders slumped. After a moment, he swallowed and nodded. "I know I can't go with you, that you need to get moving before a drone spots me. I'll stay here … fight them when they get here, or just wait for the cannons. Either way, I'm dead. I know that." His voice quavered and she barely heard the last words.

She slowly shook her head back and forth. "We've got to assume they've been tracking us since the chip went toes up. I need you to lead them off. Give me time to get some distance between the platoon and them." She placed a hand on his shoulder. "Make what happens count."

He turned his head away from her. "You're right. Of course, you're right."

Siengha began to leave but stopped herself. Dropping to one knee, she searched his face. "Do you have people? At home?"

"My brother and grandparents live on Barribes. Mother and father are gone. They were soldiers, too."

"I'll let them know."

His back straightened. "Thank you, Sergeant Siengha." He reached out his hand and she clasped it. The young officer nodded toward the group of soldiers gathering on the other side of the small open area. "You make whatever happens count, too."

"Always." She got up and turned away from him, flipping her comm channel to the platoon net. "Lieutenant's armor has a glitch, he's going to hang back. We're moving."

Flight Officer Caviness had never seen so many Vyp fighters.

From the concerned and surprised yelps of her squadron and wing mates on the net, no one else had either. After months of nearly empty space and no action it was as if some giant conduit from the Vyp side of the galaxy had been opened and all the aliens building up behind that blockage were bursting into their battlezone.

Where have they been until now? she thought.

Her hands and feet moved smoothly across the control surfaces as she twisted her fighter to the left and down, trying to avoid the arcing shots of at least five aliens. Caviness immediately changed course again, knowing instinctively that spending more than a millisecond on level flight would be disastrous. The targeting reticle flashed green then red then green again as Vyp fighters streaked across her viewscreen. She gave up trying to target individual aliens and just held her thumb on the firing touchpad, sending streams of charged slugs out.

A red flashing light appeared on the viewscreen, and at the same time a harsh tone cut through the comm chatter in her earpiece: weapons system high temp warning. Rivulets of sweat ran down both sides of her face as she stopped firing and worked the controls, turning her fighter this way and that while she searched for a bit of open space to compose herself and figure out how to deal with the swarm of aliens.

"Control, this is White Echo Three Five, I'm done. Display is red." That was Bischolov, in the flight control unit to her left. She had no time to spare a glance in his direction but her eyes briefly widened as he added: "You already know that."

As more ships were destroyed she heard pilots asking Control to shift their control units to the replacement fighters launched as soon as contact was made with the Vyp horde. Control's reply was a reminder that it was standard procedure to wait until replacement fighters were less than ten minutes from the battlezone.

But then something unheard of happened: a woman

identifying herself as Air Group Ops came on the station net, ordering all Control points to immediately release replacements fighters to available pilots.

The sweat on her face turned icy cold as Group Ops continued: "All stations! A large force of enemy fighters has broken through and is headed inbound. ETA thirty minutes. All Control points direct fighters back to the station to establish a defensive line. Launch Stations, we need every available fighter as soon as possible."

Caviness spared a glance at the navigation inset on her main display and silently groaned. Her evasive maneuvers placed the main Vyp group between her and the station: she would have to fight her way back through the massed alien ships and then outrun them.

A bluish-green stream of shells crossed her viewscreen and she snapped her fighter down and into a rolling turn, firing her own cannon at the Vyps flashing by.

Damn it! Keep moving!

Without leveling out she reversed the turn and climbed, sending her fighter in the direction she needed to go. Working the control surfaces, firing whenever the targeting reticle flashed green, she was in the heart of the alien fleet when her luck ran out.

She saw two Vyp fighters collide out of the corner of her eye and then a stream of alien fire passed over the top of her, tearing into another Vyp.

There's so many of them they can't help hitting each other!

She sent her fighter into a steep dive but before she could make another move a warning tone warbled in her earpiece, telling her the fighter was taking fire. Seconds later the blackness of space disappeared from her viewscreen, replaced by solid maroon.

Her fighter was gone. For a moment she sat in the control unit, conscious only of the ragged sound of her own breathing. When the comms crackled in her ears she jumped a little and felt the belts on the pedals cutting into the tops of her feet.

"White Hotel Three Four this is Control. Shifting you to replacement ship in five, four, three, two ... shift!"

The viewscreen flashed and the dark red was replaced by the black of space, bright specks of stars shining in the distance. "This is Three Four, I have control of replacement. Standing by for vector to defensive line."

Fifteen minutes later her viewscreen was again maroon.

Caviness and the other pilots in replacement fighters had flown head-on at maximum speed toward a point between the station and the charging Vyp phalanx. Just before reaching this ad hoc defensive line she saw the aliens pass through it, the flashes of weapons firing and ships exploding telling her the human-controlled fighters already there had been swept aside.

She and the others tried to blunt this assault, flying into the mass of enemy ships with lines of green slugs arcing out in front of them. Twisting and turning, resorting to once again holding the firing key down until the overheat warning sounded, Caviness used every trick she knew to keep her fighter in one piece. For the briefest moment the Vyp charge seemed to slow as the aliens responded to the assault, then the weight of their numbers began to tell.

Caviness heard first one, then two, and then many pilots on the comms requesting replacement ships. Diving and climbing, turning and rolling, she tried to avoid their fate but suddenly her viewscreen filled up with alien fighters and then it flashed to dark red. She gritted her teeth and yelled, hammering either side of the cockpit with her hands.

With tears of frustration joining the sweat on her face, she took a deep breath. "Control, this is Three Four requesting transfer to replacement fighter."

Several seconds passed and she was about to repeat the request when her earpiece crackled to life. "Negative your request, Three Four. No replacements available."

"Control, how long until a replacement is available."

"Three Four, there, ah, there are no more replacement fighters." She heard a sigh from the woman. "Repeat, no replacement fighters are available. Three Four, exit your unit and stand by for instruction."

Caviness stared at the red viewscreen, the enormity of the situation sinking in for the first time. After her squadron launched as part of the all-station alert she focused solely on flying and fighting the Vyps. From her seat she realized the situation was grim — *There were just so many Vyps!* — and heard a lot of pilots reporting their ships blown up ... but finding the station out of fighters left her dazed and nauseous.

She'd lost her share of fighters since joining the squadron, but those losses seemed isolated, a pittance measured against the large number of enemy fighters shot down during the same engagements. Powering down the control unit, she realized she'd never seen the losing end of a battle.

Her hands felt numb and fat as she loosened the safety belts holding her feet to the control pedals. Shakily, she stepped out onto the flight deck. To her left and right were pilots who looked just as disoriented as she felt, standing next to their vacated control units. Caviness pulled off her helmet, holding it awkwardly with both hands.

"What do we do now?" Bischolov asked no one in particular.

Caviness looked around. "The support officers should be here. They'll tell us what to do."

"Where are the support officers? Where are they?" The voice, coming from somewhere to her right, was shrill.

There was a flicker to her left and Caviness realized it was the exterior viewscreen above Tyko's control unit. Watching him dodge and fight Vyps, a pang of guilt swept through her: she hadn't thought of him since they were called to the flight deck midway through lunch. She placed her helmet on the deck and walked over to Tyko's unit, joining a knot of pilots watching him battle.

She glanced around the flight deck and realized Tyko was the last pilot from Third Wing still flying There were just too many aliens for one pilot, though, and soon his screen was red. He climbed out and pushed his way through the crowd to grab her in a tight embrace.

"Now what?" He whispered in her ear, his sweaty cheek against hers. She mutely shook her head, sagging against him.

They stood that way for what seemed to Caviness to be a long time, with many other pilots milling around them. Tyko spoke to a few of them, asking if they had seen the support officers or heard anything from their squadrons or the Wing. No one knew more than to wait for further instructions.

Those instructions came a short time later in the form of an announcement broadcast to the entire station.

"All points, attention, this is the Air Group commander. All of our fighters have been destroyed. In a few minutes the station will come under attack by a large enemy force. We have limited self-defense capabilities that I don't expect will stand up to the numbers we're facing."

There was a soft click as the comm channel cut out, then suddenly the commander was back, his voice softer. "Therefore,

I am ordering the station be evacuated. There are survival pods located on every deck, and when I'm done you should head to them in an orderly fashion. The closest habitable planets have been uploaded to each pod's guidance unit. I will not lie to you: we have no way of knowing if the, ah, if the enemy will fire on the pods, or not. But remaining on the station means certain death. Good luck to you all. It has been a pleasure to serve with you."

Caviness barely heard the commander's final words as bedlam erupted on the flight deck. Pilots began streaming toward the entrance hatch, heading to the escape pods lining the passageway outside. A knot of support officers suddenly appeared — evidently they had been waiting in the passageway, likely given advance notice of the impending evacuation order — but their shouted instructions to form up by squadron were barely audible over the hoarse voices of panicked pilots.

Tyko began shouting as well, calling the names of pilots from his squadron who were nearby. He frantically gestured to anyone looking his way, waving his arms to draw them closer. Without knowing what he was doing, Caviness joined in, calling out to get the attention of the pilots around them.

"Hey! Come over here! You! Yes, come here! Now. I need your help!" Tyko's voice boomed and she felt him taking in deep breaths. "Hey! Over here! Now! Come over here!"

Most pilots ignored their cries but five, three boys and two girls, fought against the flow of people to form a small group around them.

Tyko nodded at them. "There are some officers who may need help evacuating. Come with me!"

He led them across the flight deck to the door to Pri-Fly. It was locked from the inside, but Tyko hammered on the metal door until it suddenly opened inward. He grabbed her arm and pulled her through the doorway as the others followed.

"Flight officer, what the hell are you doing? Get these people to the escape pods!" A woman with a prosthetic leg from the thigh down stood at a console near the door. Pri-Fly was dimly lit by several rows of consoles, but Caviness saw about a dozen faces turned toward them.

"Yes, ma'am! We were wondering if your folks needed an escort to the pods." Tyko's voice was calm, almost conversational.

The woman, who wore the silver flashes of a lieutenant,

shook her head. "That won't be necessary. We're part of the station's self-defense, we'll be—" A man's voice shouting from deeper in the compartment cut her off.

"Incoming! Fifteen fighters crossing into the defense zone. I have solutions on all of them."

"Fire!"

"Missiles away!"

The lieutenant turned back to Tyko and the other pilots, her face twisted into a bitter smile. "The commander should have just given the evac order instead of being so pleased to serve with us. Wasted at least a minute."

"Fourteen kills! Engaging the leaker!" Caviness searched for the man who fired the missiles, finding him in one corner. He had thick scars on one side of his face and a prosthetic arm. "A bigger wave crossing into the defense zone. Twenty, no ... fifty. More just outside the zone, incoming."

"Weapons free. Fire when you have high-probability solutions but try to hold a few back."

"Aye, aye."

"All self-defense stations reporting contacts," called out a seated woman with one natural arm. "Large waves of fighters approaching the station from all directions!"

Caviness reached out and touched the lieutenant's sleeve. "Ma'am? How many missiles are there?"

The woman shook her head. "Not enough by half. You people really need to get to the pods."

Tyko nodded and turned to the other pilots. He opened his mouth but before he could say anything Caviness felt a series of vibrations through the deck, followed immediately by a loud metallic tearing sound.

"Hull breach! Station integrity has been compromised!" More vibrations and screeching noises, with several thuds and then a sharp clicking sound coming from the Pri-Fly door behind them. "Automatic measures activated to seal breaches."

One of the pilots tried the door handle. She turned to Tyko with a surprised look. "We're locked in!"

"The flight deck outside that door is now open to space." The lieutenant pulled Tyko's arm with one hand while pointing to a metal staircase against the far bulkhead with the other. "There are two evac pods in our berthing. Take your people ... anyone else who wants to go, can go. You've done what you can here." She addressed the last two sentences to the officers at the consoles.

Tyko reached out to grab the frightened pilots by the door. "Help them get to the pods!" He shoved them at the control officers, many of whom were struggling to attach artificial limbs taken off for comfort during what they expected would be a long but unexceptional shift.

More screeching noises echoed and the compartment vibrated and shook as the young pilots and officers hurried up the stairs. In seconds, Pri-Fly was empty except for the lieutenant, Tyko, Caviness and the officer manning the missile console.

"Are you sure you won't come with us?" Tyko looked at the lieutenant.

"No, Janewicz still has a few missiles left. We'll try to keep them interested in us, hopefully they're letting the pods go." Her face creased into a mirthless smile, and Caviness thought she looked exhausted. "Thank you for coming in, helping my people. I'd put you in for a medal or something, but ... well. Get going and good luck to you both."

Tyko nodded but the officer had already turned away. He and Caviness looked at Janewicz and she saw fear in the man's scarred face as the compartment began to shake again, more violently than just moments before. There was a shriek of rending metal and Tyko suddenly lunged forward and grabbed the lieutenant around the waist, lifting her up and over one shoulder.

"Help him!" He carried the squirming and shouting lieutenant to the stairs and began climbing.

She ran to the console where Janewicz was struggling to get up with his one good hand. Her heart began to sink as she noticed for the first time his prosthetic legs. "Can you walk? We need to move, now!"

Janewicz's artificial feet found purchase on the deck and he let out a guttural shout before shoving Caviness toward the stairs. "Go! Or I'll run you over and leave you behind!"

Reaching the next deck up, she turned to help him and side-by-side they ran down a short passageway lined by doors. Ahead of them, Tyko shrugged the now-quiet Lieutenant off his shoulder and pushed her through a round hatch. He turned to Caviness and Janewicz, waving his arm and yelling but she couldn't make out what he said over the noise of the station breaking apart.

The first pod launched as Tyko followed Caviness through the airlock to the second pod. They tumbled into seats and strapped in, with Caviness next to the quietly crying lieutenant; whether the officer was happy or sad was something she couldn't tell. Then a voice from the front yelled for everyone to hold on.

The pod detached from the station with a jolt, floating free for a moment before the drive system engaged.

Caviness looked down and saw her hand entwined with Tyko's, although she didn't remember doing it. Feeling more tired than she ever had, she glanced at the chronometer on her wrist and saw less than ten minutes had passed since she climbed from her control unit. Leaning back, she looked at Tyko. His unfocused eyes stared across the pod and when she gave his hand a squeeze, he started and turned to her.

She searched his face for a moment, then mouthed "I love you."

It was the first time she said the words to him, but Tyko didn't see it. He had turned his head and was staring blankly at the bulkhead.

WHAT HAPPENS

Sergeant Siengha sat with her back against the Ops Center bulkhead, slowly chewing a bite from the ration bar held loosely in one dirty hand. She gave no indication of hearing the drumbeat of Vyp cannon fire raining down on Operating Post Tango-5. The non-stop concussive blast waves made everything in the outpost shake and pitch: equipment, people and structures jumped, swayed and wiggled as if nudged by ghosts.

Day 11, same as Day 10, same as 9, she thought. *Right down the line.*

She sensed someone standing over her and glanced up to see Captain Oshiro. "East wall's down to a squad and a half," she said as a greeting after he pulled off his helmet. "North's not much better."

The outpost walls were standard armored pre-fab, with built-in ports for a pair of remote-operated heavy weapons that traversed on rails. At the base of the walls were bunkers for the soldiers operating the weapons and those standing by to repel attackers. Because the outpost backed up to a steep ravine the south wall was basically undefended outwards — Vyps weren't great climbers — but it still factored into the post's defense as a last-stand fallback position.

Three buildings were inside the walled perimeter — armory, Ops Center, and barracks/mess, from smallest to largest — sunk into holes blasted in the rocky ground until just a couple feet of bulkhead and armored rooftops were visible. Between the armory and south wall was a landing pad large enough for two transports; an armored enclosure on the pad was used to store drones.

Months earlier, when New Earth's forces were on the march in this part of Neptec-2, Expeditionary Corps engineers put up the outpost in a little more than twelve hours. Oshiro was the commander of the engineering unit and had been left in command of the small garrison force after the brigade marched out in search of the Vyps — a mission ending with the ambush at the Towers.

The captain nodded tiredly as he slid down next to Siengha. His helmet hit the deck with a dull thud. "Can we pull some from the west side?"

"Already in motion. Sent the drone jockeys out, too. Last drone went toes up." She offered him what was left of the ration bar. "You should eat something, sir."

"Good … and good call on the drone team." He took the bar and bit off half of what was left. "Why aren't you an officer, Siengha? Been meaning to ask."

"They tried, couple times. Turned it down."

That brought a smile to the captain's face. "Bet Command loved that."

"They got over it." She shrugged. "I just didn't need it."

"What?"

"The glamour."

Oshiro barked sudden laughter, spitting crumbs from his mouth. When he quieted, Siengha continued, staring straight ahead. "I'm better where I am."

The captain nodded. "I'm glad you're here, sergeant, but I think before this is over you'll wish you were on the other side of the galaxy."

She said nothing in reply, having long ago realized there was no point wasting time or effort wishing for something different than what was currently happening. No matter how bad the situation, Siengha knew her best chance of surviving, and by extension the best hope for everyone else around her, was to remain focused on the task at hand.

Oshiro sighed and popped the rest of the ration bar into his mouth. After swallowing, he pulled a datapad from his carrypack and tapped the screen. "I make it ten days before we run out of those, have to start eating our belts."

Siengha nodded slowly. "Perimeter turrets will run out of shells long before that."

The captain sighed again. "Yeah. How did we get into this mess again?"

The sergeant studied Oshiro out of the corner of her eye. She'd been impressed with the engineering officer's calm demeanor and willingness to let her take the lead on tactical matters, but she wondered if he was beginning to truly comprehend how bad the situation was.

Retreating from the Towers battle, Siengha and what was left of her platoon linked up other survivors at a rally point about two days march from the outpost. Promised air support was absent — untold masses of aliens were attacking everywhere on Neptec-2 — and Vyp drones immediately spotted the concentration of humans. Cannon and missile fire raked the survivors at the rally point and nearly every step along the way to the relative safety of OP Tango-5.

The fire was so thick Siengha assumed the only time the column wasn't being hit was when the Vyps were reloading.

The senior officer, a major from brigade staff, and two captains were killed the morning of the second day by a missile explosion, leaving three fairly green lieutenants and a handful of non-commissioned officers to lead fifty-eight soldiers through the outpost main gate.

Fifty-eight out of the five hundred who marched to the Towers.

Once inside the outpost, they learned the status of New Earth forces was critical across the planet and above it. Communication with other units was intermittent as the Vyps hammered through defensive lines and destroyed whole formations. More troubling, Oshiro reported having lost contact with the fleet of logistics and command ships in orbit about the same time the brigade was attacked at the Towers.

The third day after Siengha returned to the outpost they received a redirected message from Expeditionary Corps Command on Neptec-1 informing all subordinate units the Vyptellian offensive was galaxy-wide, not just limited to their system. All units were directed to defend their positions as a counterattack was being organized to regain lost territory.

Listening to the broadcast in the Ops Center with the outpost's few officers and non-coms, volume turned up because of cannon and missile explosions, Siengha saw worried and disbelieving looks exchanged all around. It was then that she suggested constructing the south wall redoubt, partly as a way to keep people busy but also because the need for a last stand position seemed a foregone conclusion.

The south wall defense turrets were turned to face inward, a field modification requiring a lot of improvisation by Oshiro and his engineers. At the same time, an escape hatch was cut to allow access to the narrow strip of level ground between the outer wall and the edge of the ravine. Ropes were attached to the wall face and left coiled, ready to be kicked over the side — rappelling to the floor of the ravine represented the final option for any survivors.

All the while Vyp drones circled overhead, directing cannon and missile fire down onto the post. The outpost's anti-air weapons knocked many down, but the aliens had plenty to spare and one by one the air defense launchers were targeted and taken out.

Armor in the walls, buildings, bunkers and their own suits kept the soldiers safe enough, in theory. But after days of continuous bombardment their nerves were rattled and judgment clouded. The slightest mistake — an unsecured hatch or viewport, zigging instead of zagging on open ground, not buttoning up after hygiene or food breaks — resulted in catastrophe.

Casualties steadily mounted and the post's leadership was especially hard hit: two lieutenants were killed within hours of each other while checking perimeter positions on the sixth day. A day later a salvo of missiles exploding above the landing pad made Siengha the senior sergeant.

Oshiro wanted her to remain in the Ops Center with him, but she wouldn't hear of it. The soldiers on the perimeter and the quick reaction force standing by in the armory needed more than hourly net checks; left isolated their already battered spirits could turn to panic. So she spent much of the day moving around the post, varying routes to spend as little time in the open as possible while visiting the two soldiers guarding the south wall redoubt, the squads stationed in the other three walls, and the quick reaction team.

She listened to their complaints, got them what they needed if she could, and above all tried to bolster their courage. Wherever she went the soldiers wanted to know the same thing: *When will the Vyps attack?*

Siengha didn't have answer for them. She had a few ideas, though.

The outpost was completely cut off and now far behind the leading edge of the alien advance, so it was possible the Vyps planned to reduce the outpost's defenders through cannon and missile fire before assaulting. Or, perhaps the aliens intended on starving them out, knowing any type of relief operation was unlikely as the New Earth forces on planet were in disarray.

Such tactics would make sense from a human commander seeking to minimize casualties, but the Vyps had never displayed such concerns in the past. Then again, the aliens had never mounted a galaxy-wide attack before.

"Capt'n! Sergeant! West wall sensors show movement." The corporal on comms duty at the tactical display swiveled around to face them. "North wall now also has movement. Danger close for both."

Siengha and Oshiro scrambled to their feet, pulling their helmets on at the same time. Lowering the faceshield, she switched her comm to the perimeter net and her earpiece relayed a babble of excited voices; without drone surveillance the Vyps were able to get within yards of the wall before sensors detected them.

"All stations, Papa Sierra! Quiet on the net," she commanded. "Keep reports short and understandable. Calm down."

She stood next to Oshiro at the tactical display, watching as two sets of red triangles drew closer to the green lines representing the north and west walls. Moments later the ripping sound of the automatic turrets firing joined the noise of exploding cannon shells.

"West wall, north wall. Fire and move. Short bursts. Conserve shells, make 'em count." Siengha paused for a moment. "East wall, stay alert. Eyes front."

"Are they probing or is this it?" Oshiro's voice on the command net in her left ear.

"Probably probing, but could be a feint. We'll know if business picks up on east wall."

"Sergeant! Vyp cannons have stopped!" The corporal's voice on the command net was shrill. She was about to tell him to calm down when the perimeter net crackled in her right ear: east wall sensors had movement, danger close.

"All stations, Papa Sierra. Stand by for attack in force. I say again, stand by for attack in force."

She was wrong, though, as the Vyptellians continued to employ tactics previously unseen. For forty minutes the aliens tested the outpost's defenses, moving small teams forward and then back, against one wall and then another. Next they probed two walls simultaneously, with different sized groups, and then all three walls at once. At that point the cannonade began again, leading Siengha to wonder whether an all-out assault was coming or if the Vyps were simply gathering information while the humans burned off ammo.

She was about to order a phased resupply of the walls when

a large group of Vyps approached the corner where the west and north walls joined. Turrets on both walls moved to engage as an even larger group appeared on the tactical display at the west wall's midpoint. The jackhammer sound of heavy weapons was once again heard in the Ops Center over the deeper drumbeat of cannon explosions.

But what at first glance seemed to be just another test of the outpost's defenses proved to be much more.

Although turret crews were rotated between Vyp probes, the men and women guarding the walls had been tired and edgy even before the first alien assault. Now, as the initial surge of adrenaline faded they began to make mistakes. Weapons were fired before targets were in range or for longer than necessary, wasting shells and raising system temperatures; turrets were moved predictably between the same points or remained in one position too long.

This last error lost the outpost, and the end came quickly.

As the two turrets near the northwest corner engaged the enemy to their front, a salvo of two dozen rockets from portable launchers slammed into the other turret near the west wall's midpoint, which was firing at the large group in front of it. But rather than remaining in near constant motion, the turret operator left the weapon stationary for too many seconds. More than twenty rockets slammed into the turret, disabling the traverse mechanism and freezing the weapon in place.

Hearing the report over the perimeter net, Siengha instantly recognized the danger: about a third of the west wall was no longer covered by a heavy weapon, giving the Vyps a clear path into the outpost. Turning away from the tactical display, she picked up her assault rifle and checked the magazine. She looked at Oshiro.

"Watch the other walls but be ready to run."

Switching to the perimeter net as she ran out of the Ops Center, Siengha ordered the quick reaction force to the west wall. She had placed the last green lieutenant in charge of the twenty-five soldier QRF and now silently hoped the young woman wouldn't falter.

Rounding the corner of the Ops Center, she got her first view of the wall as the Vyp cannonade stopped. Aliens were pouring over the twelve-foot wall like water through a breached dam, landing with dull thuds on the grated walkway attached two-thirds of the way up. A handful of human soldiers stood at the base of the wall, firing assault rifles up at the aliens, but as Siengha watched a group of Vyps jumped to the ground around them.

Screams echoed through the perimeter net in her ear as the QRF arrived. She quickly arranged them into two firing lines, one prone and the other kneeling. The QRF fired volleys of charged rifle shells into the Vyps (and, she realized fleetingly, any human survivors of the wall breach) and for a brief moment Siengha thought they may stem the tide.

But the stream of aliens crossing the wall didn't slow and Vyps began to move laterally on the walkways, flanking the QRF and infiltrating the rest of the outpost.

"All stations, Papa Sierra. Execute fall back plan. I say again, execute fall back plan."

Any hope of an orderly retreat to the redoubt in the south wall was overcome by the swiftly moving Vyptellians. Oshiro and the corporal on comm guard were killed when five aliens burst into the Ops Center with weapons firing. The squads manning turrets in the other walls were attacked from behind, with just a handful escaping as alien sappers tossed bundled explosives into their bunkers.

Led by Siengha and the outpost's last officer, the QRF executed a firing retreat, holding the aliens to their front at bay with massed volleys. They nearly made it to the south wall before a large group of Vyps slammed into them from one side, shattering the two firing lines into a confused mass as aliens and humans fought hand-to-hand.

Ducking under swinging alien weapons, Siengha escaped the melee and ran for the redoubt, dodging marauding Vyps coming at her from all directions. Instinctively, she realized the outpost's defenders were no longer an organized unit she could command. Each was on his or her own.

Approaching the south wall, lines of green tracers reached out at her like thin fingers. She heard the crack as the slugs flew past and then grunts and hisses as they tore into Vyp bodies. A handful of soldiers had made it to the redoubt and were providing covering fire. Throwing herself into the nearest bunker, she turned and saw no living humans among the mass of aliens surging toward the redoubt. She grabbed the nearest soldier by the shoulder and pointed to the access hatch through the wall.

"Go! Down the rope! Go!"

Siengha brought her rifle up and began firing into the mass of Vyps while the others escaped through the hatch. When everyone else was out of the bunker, Siengha passed through the hatch and slammed it shut. She found one soldier left on the narrow ledge beyond the wall. He was hooked up to the rope but made no move to descend into the darkness of the ravine. He turned to her with wild eyes.

"What if there are Vyps down there, too?"

Without saying a word she shoved him off the ledge. The soldier cried out as he grabbed at the rope and began sliding down.

What happens, happens, she thought, hooking herself to the rope and stepping off the ledge.

A PROMISE KEPT

The Barribes space port security guard recognized Siengha on sight. Not *who* she was, of course, *what* she was.

"Welcome back," he told her and she nodded in reply. The guard, a man in his mid-twenties, wore over his heart on the dark blue uniform a small orange ribbon indicating he was a war veteran.

They were standing next to a gate for ships coming in from outside the system. He offered to take her small carrypack but she refused with a head shake. The guard seemed to take no offense, falling into step with her as she searched for an exit from the cavernous arrivals hall. He pointed to an archway and she grunted her thanks.

"Look, I know you've been in hours of counseling sessions and have had your fill of being told how things are now in the home system," he said quietly, leaning his head in close to hers. "But give me a minute of your time, have a coffee with me before you head out, okay?"

They passed through the archway into the space port's main hall and she stopped, overwhelmed by the sight of it. It was even larger than the arrivals hall and seemed alive — all shining metal and glass walls lined with flashing viewscreens and thousands of people of all sizes and shapes, wearing clothing of every color in the spectrum, hurrying to and fro past kiosks and shops selling all manner of goods.

The guard gently touched her elbow, guiding her in the direction of a small cafe just outside the arrivals hall entrance. "War's been over five years now," he said apologetically. "Come on. First cup is on me."

He pointed her to a small table in one corner before ordering two mugs of steaming black coffee at the counter. The guard set the mugs on the table and sat down across from her.

"I was one of the first, before they started the processing centers." He wrapped his hands around the mug and stared down into the black liquid. "My father met me and we had a coffee, right here. Cost a lot more then, too."

The man smiled faintly at the memory before glancing up at

Siengha. "Anyway, now I keep my eyes open on shift, try to pull you aside when you get here. Haven't been many the past couple years. Most everyone is already back by now, I guess. Those who are coming back."

She nodded and took a sip from the mug. The coffee was hot and flavorful, much better than the leftover field rations at the processing center and heavenly compared to what they had brewed for themselves while hiding out on Neptec-2. She looked through the cafe entrance at the bustling space port. "Doesn't seem real, but I suppose everyone tells you that."

He shrugged, apparently not wanting to minimize what she was experiencing. "I struggled with it, too. They were just coming off the war economy when I got back, so there was still rationing and not everything was available. Back then, you could tell there had been a war. Now ... well, I'm sure they told you, most people won't ask and don't want to know. Hey, can I see your ident chip?"

He pulled a datapad from his belt and plugged in the small square issued at the processing center after DNA confirmation of her identity. When the guard looked up from the pad display she could see he was impressed.

"Wow, you won't have to worry about getting by for awhile, maybe ever. You're one of the very first." He detached the ident chip and pushed it back across the table. "Well, Sergeant Siengha, believe it or not you — all of us, really — have the Vyps to thank for that. The first post-war council wanted to take back our credits, use 'em to rework the economy. The Vyps said no to that." He tapped the orange ribbon on his chest. "They also let veterans represent themselves as such when everyone else wanted to just ignore what happened."

Siengha took another sip of coffee, processing what the man was saying. So many had been involved in the war. Generations, whole families, grandparents, mothers and fathers, sons and daughters. How could anyone ignore it? She could understand the people of New Earth welcoming their release from privation and the fear of losing their loved ones. But to pretend it never happened?

They finished their coffee in silence, which she appreciated. Whatever the guard wanted to impart to her, comradeship or just a soft landing on her return, he seemed content that it had been accomplished.

"Thank you for the coffee, but I have something I need to

get done." She stood and picked up her carrypack.

"Of course. I noticed you're not originally from Barribes, so I'm guessing you're looking for someone." She nodded. "Try the Veterans Ministry office, but you may have better luck with the Orange Society. It was started and is run by veterans, and a lot of us find it more helpful than the government. Hope you don't mind, I put the address on your chip."

* * * *

The young man who introduced himself as an advocacy counselor waved at a worn sofa in one corner of the room. "Please, sit down. Do you want some coffee? Tea? Water?"

Siengha shook her head as she sank into the cushions. The man grabbed a mug from his desk and topped it with black liquid from a portable machine on a table in the corner.

After easing himself down on the opposite end of the sofa, he looked at her with curiosity. "What can I do for you?"

She thought the Orange Society counselor couldn't have been much over twenty, but he carried himself as much older. Part of it was the long scars on one side of his face, but also there was a seriousness to him that reminded her of soldiers who had survived a few battles. She glanced over at his desk and saw an image frame with a younger version of the man sitting next to a beautiful dark-haired girl holding an infant.

He turned to see what she was looking at. "We met as flight officers on a base station." Running a finger over the scars on his face, the counselor continued, "Got this when the escape pod we were in landed hard. Vyps hit the station in the Big Push ... that's what they call it now. Anyway, they knocked out all our ships and were hitting the station hard, so we had to punch out. Station blew up right after."

"How long were you a pilot?"

"Three years, started at thirteen. I'm not sure we were really pilots." He smiled ruefully. "We controlled the ships remotely. First Vyps I ever saw in person was when they flew us off the planet we landed on."

"Oh?"

"Mmm. There was a couple hundred others from the station who landed with us. The Vyps passed us by so we just made do. Set up a settlement, cultivated some crops. It wasn't easy but most of us were pretty young and overdue for some hard work."

"How long were you there?"

"Couple years. We had comms, so we knew about the surrender and some wanted to come back then, but others liked what we had and wanted to stay." He laughed. "After three years on a space station, feeling dirt between your toes, jumping into a river or lake … those were hard to give up again so soon."

"I suppose so."

The man chuckled. "As a ground pounder I'm sure you never lacked for dirt to squeeze between your toes. Anyway, it took time to coordinate the transport. A lot of people were stranded across the galaxy, I'm sure you know, and at that point the Vyps weren't allowing us to have long-range ships."

"Why did you decide to come back?"

He pointed at the image frame. "Our daughter was born there but we wanted her to know any family we had left. We talked about it just being a trip, returning to the settlement after a year, but then we got here and decided it was best to stay."

"Did you have much family to introduce her to?"

"Some. More on her side here on Barribes. That's why we settled here." He set the mug on the floor at his feet. "Enough about me. How can I help you?"

"I'm looking for the family of a soldier I served with. A second lieutenant; I was his platoon sergeant." Siengha licked her lips. "He was a flight officer, too. I suppose if the war had kept going, maybe I'd been your sergeant, too."

The counselor nodded. "I was about a year from being too old to fly remotely. Why do you want to find his family?"

She sat quietly for a moment, ordering her thoughts into words. Then she told him about the retreat from the Towers. He listened quietly at first and at the point where she thought he may react, he did, his face twisting as if he'd smelled something slightly unpleasant.

At the end of the story, she added, "From your face I guess you read that book, too. At the processing center we heard the guy, Furman, was using Vyp records to write it." She shifted in her seat. Nodded. "I read it. Most of us did. We wanted to know more about them. About what happened."

He leaned forward and quietly said, "You didn't know. You couldn't know."

"No."

"You were following Command procedure, leaving h—"

"Yes."

There was silence for several moments, until she added, "I made a promise. He's listed as missing, presumed dead. His people should know more than just that."

The counselor sat back and stared at the ceiling. "Our families were told the same thing about us. Right after the surrender, things were very confused. The new Council disbanded the Military Command. So many soldiers were scattered around and comm networks were shattered. No one knew much of anything for sure. Then the Vyps returned their prisoners, which was the best news possible for some families. But not for others."

He turned to face Siengha. "We were able to get word to our families a few months after the war ended. My parents were happy, of course, but they told me it was very hard seeing one family celebrating the return of their son or daughter while next door the people sat and waited."

There was a pause as he studied her face. "You know, they may not want to talk to you. Even if they've accepted he's gone."

"I know."

"Give me the name and unit, I'll see what I can find out."

She waited on the couch as he accessed a data terminal on his desk and attached a comm device to one ear. Siengha sat back and let her mind wander, suddenly feeling very tired. She had been on the go since arriving on Barribes three days earlier and couldn't remember the last time she hadn't felt on edge. Without realizing it, she dropped into a shallow sleep.

"Hey, hey. Sergeant Siengha. Hey." The counselor's soft voice brought her back to wakefulness.

"Sorry," she mumbled, sitting up and quickly wiping her chin as her cheeks grew warm.

"No problem. You're not the first to find this comfortable." He patted the cushion he was sitting on. "I learned early on not to grab or shake ground pounders when they're sleeping. Nearly got my head taken off."

She smiled despite her embarrassment. "Smart."

Siengha stood up and stretched, feeling the muscles in her legs and back loosening. She walked to the coffee machine and poured some of the hot liquid into a paper cup. Turning around to face the counselor, she flexed her head from side to side until the neck bones cracked.

"How long have you been doing this?" She made a sweeping

gesture with her free hand.

"About two-and-a-half years."

"Since coming back?"

"Just about. Once we decided to stay I joined the Society." He also stood and stretched. "As I said, right after the war the new Council wanted nothing to do with the military and veterans. The Society filled a void."

"Government still wants nothing to do with us. The Veterans Ministry wasted my time."

He nodded. "Many on the Council today want to do more, but they also know how hard it will be re-gaining our trust. Veterans don't handle betrayal well. So they work with us quietly."

"Seems harder than it needs to be."

The counselor laughed. "Politics usually is." He sat back down, and his expression grew serious. "You know, it wasn't just the Council, though. People were tired of the war. It was everywhere and everything for sixteen years ... part of their jobs, in their stores and schools, in the music they listened to and the vids they watched and articles they read. They sent their kids and in some cases their grandkid off to fight. For some of us, it was all we knew."

The counselor jumped to his feet and began pacing in front of the couch. "Then it was over, and everyone was glad. They could just worry about themselves for a change, but I think they also felt guilty for being glad. So, they told us we were great, and brave, and our service was appreciated, and even after they disbanded Command the politicians always had some vets up on stage with them. But the less heard from us, the better."

He suddenly stopped pacing and exhaled. After a moment he faced her, a wry smile on his face. "Sorry."

She shook her head. "No problem."

"Look, I found what's left of the family and they're willing to meet you. The grandfather died right after the surrender, the brother said his heart gave out. They live in a farm commune about a day away by ground transport."

She nodded. "I'll leave right away."

"What are you going to say to them about how he died?"

Siengha stared into the coffee for a moment before answering. "I'll tell them the truth. That he died protecting his soldiers. I'll tell them why, too."

The counselor nodded. He reached out a hand. "Here, give

me your chip and I'll upload the address."

He took the small square back to his desk and inserted it into the data terminal. After a few keystrokes he extracted it and turned back to her. "Tell me, was this lieutenant someone special to you?"

"Not really."

The counselor handed her the chip. "I ask because I'm trying to understand why you're doing this, going to see his family after all this time."

"He asked me to."

"I know, but ... well, you served in a lot of units. Saw a lot of combat. He couldn't have been the only one to ask."

She paused, thinking back over the long years. "He wasn't."

"So. Why him?"

"He was the last one to ask." Siengha finished the coffee in one long drink and handed him the paper cup. "Thank you. What you do here is good, important. Keep it up."

* * * *

The man who answered the door was probably the same age as the Orange Society counselor, but Siengha thought he wore his years younger than the former flight officer. He ushered her into the small apartment with a nervous wave, directing her to a tidy room with a couch and several cushioned chairs.

A gray-haired woman sat on one of the chairs facing the door, and Siengha could almost feel the anticipation on her lined face. She took a seat across from the woman as the brother slipped into a chair to one side. The old woman introduced herself with a warm, soft voice and a smile, but Siengha saw tears forming in her eyes.

She took a breath and began, saying what she'd practiced over and over on the long trip back.

"My name is Sergeant Siengha, and I would like to tell you about your grandson's last day. We were on Neptec-2 and I was his platoon sergeant. Our unit was part of a large force advancing toward ..."

The End

ABOUT THE AUTHOR

Born and raised in the American Midwest, Scott Whitmore enlisted in the U.S. Navy in 1982 and was later commissioned as an officer. After retiring from military service he joined the sports staff at *The Herald*, a daily newspaper located in Everett, Wash. In 2009, his feature story about a young Everett sprint car racer was awarded third place in the annual writing contest held by the National Motorsports Press Association.

Scott left The Herald in 2009 to begin working as a freelance writer. In addition to his novels, he has written for various sports and motorsports magazines and blogs, and his profile of NASCAR driver Danica Patrick was included in the August 2011 *New York Yankees Magazine* as part of a special issue celebrating women in sports.

His previous novels are *Carpathia* and *The Devil's Harvest*. Contact him by email at 40westmedia@comcast.net or follow @ScottWhitmore on Twitter.